Billie's gaze flicked up to Alexei's bold brown profile and froze at the sight of the glisten of moisture highlighting his hard cheekbones.

Silent tears were rolling down his face. She could *taste* his sadness, his regret for times past never to be regained. Her throat thickened, her own eyes were wet, and she looked hurriedly away, feeling that she could not possibly intrude on so intensely private a moment, when he believed himself alone and unobserved. But, oh, how she longed for the right to push open that door and hurry to his side to offer him comfort! But freedom of expression was not part of her role, as such, and she reluctantly walked away while scolding herself for having underestimated the depth of Alexei's loss and his feelings. His tough self-discipline had fooled even her, persuading her that he was totally in control and that business would pretty much go on as usual.

THE DRAKOS BABY

An enthralling linked-story duet by
USA TODAY bestselling author

LYNNE GRAHAM

*A Greek billionaire with amnesia, a secret
baby, a convenient marriage…it's a recipe
for rip-roaring passion, revelations and the
reunion of a lifetime!*

Available this month:

PART ONE

The Pregnancy Shock

Available next month:

PART TWO

A Stormy Greek Marriage

Billie's baby has been born, but she hasn't
told Alexei about his son's existence. Yet when
she returns to Greece and he proposes a
marriage of convenience she knows she just
has to take her chance to be with the man she
loves. But Alexei is amazed to find his wife isn't
a virgin on their wedding night—
*and that's just the first shocking revelation in
this stormy marriage….*

Lynne Graham
THE PREGNANCY SHOCK

THE
DRAKOS
BABY

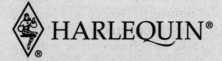

HARLEQUIN®

TORONTO • NEW YORK • LONDON
AMSTERDAM • PARIS • SYDNEY • HAMBURG
STOCKHOLM • ATHENS • TOKYO • MILAN • MADRID
PRAGUE • WARSAW • BUDAPEST • AUCKLAND

Recycling programs
for this product may
not exist in your area.

ISBN-13: 978-0-373-12951-5

THE PREGNANCY SHOCK

First North American Publication 2010.

Copyright © 2010 by Lynne Graham.

All about the author...
Lynne Graham

Born of Irish/Scottish parentage, **LYNNE GRAHAM** has lived in Northern Ireland all her life. She has one brother. She grew up in a seaside village and now lives in a country house surrounded by a woodland garden, which is wonderfully private.

Lynne first met her husband when she was fourteen. They married after she completed a degree at Edinburgh University. Lynne wrote her first book at fifteen and it was rejected everywhere. She started writing again when she was at home with her first child. It took several attempts before she sold her first book and the delight of seeing that book for sale in the local newsagents has never been forgotten.

Lynne always wanted a large family and she now has five children. Her eldest, her only natural child, is in her twenties and is a university graduate. Her other children, who are every bit as dear to her heart, are adopted: two from Sri Lanka and two from Guatemala. In Lynne's home, there is a rich and diverse cultural mix, which adds a whole extra dimension of interest and discovery to family life.

The family has two pets. Thomas, a very large and affectionate black cat, bosses the dog and hunts rabbits. The dog is Bella, an adorable Corgi. At night, dog and cat sleep together in front of the kitchen stove.

Lynne loves gardening and cooking, collects everything from old toys to rock specimens and is crazy about every aspect of Christmas.

CHAPTER ONE

ALEXEI DRAKOS broodingly surveyed the crowded Port Vauban marina from the deck of his yacht, *Sea Queen*. There were paparazzi everywhere. As a man who set a high value on privacy, he was not impressed. He was even less impressed with the topless sunbathers on the vessel moored beside his who were calling out to him and making inviting gestures. *As if*, Alexei thought with all the disdain of an aristocrat for rotten meat. As a teenager he had sampled many female bodies without the need to make dates or chit-chat, but he had grown up since then.

If Calisto had not begged him to bring her to Cannes, he would have been miles away from the noise, the poseurs and the fuss. *Sea Queen* was easily the biggest, sleekest and most expensive yacht there but, as he was a fourth generation Drakos, and possessed of fabulous wealth and privilege from birth, such petty comparisons were beneath Alexei's arrogant notice.

Standing six feet four inches in his bare feet, Alexei was built with the lean muscular power of a trained athlete and surprisingly fit for a noted workaholic. Half Russian and half Greek, he was a dazzlingly handsome man with a formidable reputation as a womaniser. Yet for the past few months there had been only *one* woman in his life: Calisto, the ex-wife of the Swiss electronics tycoon, Xavier Bethune. Keen to get back to work and aware that his business team awaited him indoors, Alexei strode back into his on-board office, which was as streamlined and technologically advanced as any on shore.

Some minutes later, Calisto stalked into the crowded room without warning. Alexei was surprised, for he had sent her down the coast to tour his magnificent villa in an effort to get some peace. An echoing silence spread even before Calisto burst into staccato speech. 'You won't believe what I've discovered at your villa!'

'Nothing short of the Loch Ness monster in the bath tub would excuse this intrusion when I am working,' Alexei drawled, and he was not entirely joking as he glanced up from his laptop to survey the irate blonde.

'The place is a disgrace! The swimming pool hasn't been serviced in months, the garden is overgrown and the house isn't even stocked for our stay next week,' Calisto raged, her bright blue eyes full of indignation. 'And when I asked the housekeeper to explain herself, all she would say was that Billie always dealt with that stuff and that she had received no instructions.'

Calisto Bethune was a six foot tall beauty and former model, quite capable of stopping traffic with her stunning face and shapely body. She was Greek-born, she was gorgeous and, now that she was free of her husband, the woman whom Alexei had loved and lost as a teenager was finally his again.

'Did you hear anything I just said, Alexei?' Calisto prompted impatiently. 'Last month the refit on *Sea Queen* overran and we couldn't use her. Who was responsible for that? Every place I go in your life things are going wrong and I discover that this Billie creature is at fault!'

'Until a couple of months ago, Billie took care of all my properties as well as my social calendar and travel arrangements. Unfortunately, she insisted on taking a career break and her replacement was so inept, I sacked her after a month—'

Calisto studied him wide-eyed, a frown building on her face. 'This Billie that everybody talks about is a...*woman*?'

'Why not?' Alexei returned to his laptop with renewed energy as he was hotwired to the pursuit of profit and in no mood to hear any more about boring domestic problems. No Drakos male he had ever known had concerned himself with such trivialities. In even listening to Calisto's tirade, he believed he was being very tolerant, offering the listening ear that all women were supposed to crave.

'And this Billie, this woman *insisted* on taking time off? Since when do you allow your employees to insist on anything?' Calisto demanded.

Alexei frowned and straightened before he rose to his full height and urged the gorgeous blonde across the hallway outside the office into the opulent and spacious salon. 'I've known Billie since she was a child growing up on Speros. She has a little more licence than the rest of my team—'

A frozen look stiffened Calisto's wide cheekbones. 'Does she indeed?'

'Until now Billie has always been available when I want her. *Usually* she doesn't take vacations or even days off. Day or night, she has worked extremely hard for me,' Alexei volunteered, but his tone was flat because in spite of what he was saying he too blamed Billie for the many annoying developments that had taken the edge off his comfort in recent months.

Billie Foster, his most trusted aide and gofer, his right-hand woman, had insisted on taking an eight-month-long career break to look after her recently widowed but pregnant aunt in England. His even white teeth clenched as he mentally shifted through the aggravations he'd had to tolerate during Billie's prolonged absence. Impersonal and personal matters that he had once taken for granted as being taken care of were suddenly rolling up in front of him undone and causing him *considerable* inconvenience.

He had never dreamt that Billie might act in so selfish a manner. Even though she knew he disagreed with her taking such a lengthy break, she had gone ahead regardless. He had been too soft with her. He should have told her *no*. He should have told her that if she left she would have no job to return to. After all, for what did he pay her such a handsome salary? To go running off to England whenever she took the fancy? Alexei had expected a lot more from a young woman whom he had known since childhood and who owed more than she knew to his family's generosity.

'A wife would take charge of your properties and your social calendar. It would be no big deal,' Calisto remarked softly. 'Then you wouldn't need a Billie in your life.'

Alexei was too clever and wary of feminine manipulation to respond. He shrugged a broad shoulder and signalled a steward to bring coffee. Calisto might be the first woman to spend more than a few weeks with him, but marriage was another step altogether in his book. He was all too well aware of how expensive a bad marriage could be: his late father had endured three very nasty and costly divorces. No, Alexei was in no hurry to name the day. Although Calisto was the first to even consider that the altar might be within her sights, she might also yet reveal a deal-breaking flaw. In his experience, women were rarely predictable and even more rarely truthful.

Turning her nose up at the coffee that powered Alexei through his long working day, Calisto put on some music and began to dance, twisting and working her hips in movements as suggestive as any lap dancer's. Recognising that she was trying to use sex to get his attention, Alexei studiously ignored her while wondering why she thought a lap-dancing impression might get her up the aisle. If anything the demonstration repelled him. Outside the bedroom a wife should have a certain dignity, he reflected seriously, adding that quality to the mental list he cherished. Under the influence of a few drinks at a party, Calisto could well become an embarrassment.

A brilliantly coloured print scarf lying on a bar stool caught his attention. Black brows pleating, he lifted it up. It belonged to Billie, who had little sense of colour

coordination. A faint old-fashioned peachy scent that
was familiar assailed him and his nostrils flared. Just as
quickly, his penetrating dark eyes took on a frowning
expression of bewilderment. The sense of something
erotic skimmed indistinctly through his mind and his
body reacted with primal male hunger, hardening with
instant lust. Bemused by that powerful reaction and
unable to find a logical connection, Alexei registered
that he was still holding the scarf. Filled with distaste
at the tenor of his thoughts, for there could be no woman
more sexually naïve than Billie, he tossed the material
down again…

'You'll miss all the options here…' As the two women
emerged from the public library Billie waved a hand to
encompass the busy London street, full of shops, res-
taurants and bustling traffic. 'That you should return to
Greece with me seemed such a great idea after John
died, but now I feel horribly guilty for getting you
involved in all this. The island is very quiet—'

'You're just tired and feeling down again,' Hilary
scolded, a tall, slender blonde with gentle brown eyes in
her late thirties. She bore little resemblance to her di-
minutive red-headed niece with her emerald-green gaze,
whose heavily pregnant state made her seem almost as
wide as she was tall. She urged the younger woman onto
the bus and passed the journey with a cheerful monologue
about how much she hated the damp English climate and
how much she was looking forward to having the peace
to write the book she had long been planning.

Billie, who was more tired than she was prepared to

admit, remained unconvinced. In an attempt to do the best she could for her own future and her baby's she had ensnared Hilary in her plans but she felt increasingly guilty about that fact. It was a relief, however, to return to her aunt's comfortable semi-detached house and sit down with a cup of tea.

'You just don't appreciate how desperate I am for a change of scene and direction and I couldn't afford either without your support,' the blonde woman declared ruefully. 'Without your financial assistance during John's illness, I wouldn't even still be living in this house. Your generosity made it possible for us to stay here until he had to go into care; being able to be some-where familiar helped John a good deal because he couldn't cope with change.'

Hilary's voice cracked up a little because her husband had only passed away some months earlier. As a result of early-onset dementia, the essence of John's person-ality had gone long before he'd died at the age of forty-three in a care home. Towards the end, as his condition had worsened, he had become too difficult for his wife to look after alone. Prior to that, Hilary had supported her husband for several years and had had to give up working as a teacher to do so. The welfare benefits the couple were entitled to had been too meagre to meet their mortgage payments and Billie had come willingly to the rescue to ease their plight.

'I was glad to help,' Billie told the woman who had often been the only voice of sanity during her childhood, even though they had lived so far part.

Billie's mother, Lauren, had moved to the Greek

island of Speros when Billie was only eight years old. Lauren had always been an irresponsible parent, who'd put the latest man in her life ahead of her child's needs. More often than Billie cared to remember, a visit or a phone call from her flighty parent's sensible sister, Hilary, had persuaded Lauren to behave more like a normal mother.

Hilary groaned, 'Unfortunately you helped all of us too much for your own good. You bought a house for your mother, you gave John and I an allowance—'

'And, all on my own, I spent a foolish fortune building my own house on Speros too,' Billie cut in, uncomfortable with the other woman's gratitude. 'If only I had thought ahead to a time when I might not want to work for Alexei any more. If only I had just put all that money in the bank instead...'

'Nobody has a crystal ball. You may not feel it right now but you are still very young at twenty-six,' Hilary reasoned soothingly. 'You had a great job and you were earning a small fortune, so you had no reason to fear the future.'

Billie's delicate features shadowed. She would not be comforted on that score for she blamed herself bitterly for her extravagance. She had grown up in poverty, had lived through the experience of going hungry at mealtimes and of hiding from view when the landlord called for his rent. With those memories behind her, she believed she should have saved up for the proverbial rainy day.

'Nor should you have any reason to fear the future now. Your baby's father is a very rich man,' Hilary pointed out firmly.

Billie's hands clenched into the tissue she was

holding. 'I think I'd rather be dead than face Alexei like this. Thank heaven I was out at a hospital appointment the day he called here at the house to see me!'

'Yes, we weren't expecting that. Fortunately he wouldn't come in, so I doubt if he had the time or the presence of mind to notice that I didn't actually look very pregnant,' Hilary remarked wryly.

Billie was still engaged in recalling her shock on learning that Alexei, over in London on business, had decided to visit her without so much as a phone call to forewarn her of his plans. How shocked he would have been had she answered the door to him with an obviously pregnant stomach! It was pure luck that the deception she had entered into with Hilary—the planned pretence that her aunt was the one having the baby—had not been exposed on the spot. Afterwards, she had phoned him to ask if there was something he had needed her assistance with and he had laughed and said that his visit had been a last minute idea, taken when he had some time to use up before heading to the airport and his flight home.

'If you ever feel in need of courage to face Alexei Drakos, I would face him for you.' Hilary said this softly but the light of battle was in her usually placid gaze.

Billie lifted her chin. 'It's not a matter of being too scared—'

'Oh, I know you're not scared of Alexei Drakos. But you're still madly in love with him and determined to protect him from the consequences of his own behaviour.'

Her colour fluctuating, Billie said sharply, 'It's not like that. I have my pride and my plans. I don't need him in any way. If I continue to work for Alexei for at least a year after my baby's born, I'll be able to save up enough capital to start up my own business back here.'

Hilary gritted her teeth on a tart retort because she didn't want to upset Billie. Her niece, after all, had already suffered the considerable trauma of watching the father of her child—and the man she loved—fall for an old flame from his past. Even so, Billie's reasons for remaining silent were insufficient to satisfy Hilary's hunger for natural justice. So Alexei Drakos had bedded Billie, an employee, one dark night, had recklessly ignored the need to use protection and had conveniently contrived to forget the entire episode by the next day? Did pigs fly too? Hilary's only loyalty was to Billie and she was a cynic who would, had the decision been up to her, have happily destroyed Alexei's latest liaison with a public announcement of Billie's fecund state.

That same evening Billie went into labour. She was a week early and, in spite of all the prenatal classes she had diligently attended, she almost panicked when she awakened and realised what was happening to her. Her case was packed, everything prepared for the big event. She was thoroughly fed up with hauling round her huge bump and trying to sleep while a very lively baby seemed to be trying to kick its way out during the night. But there was also a great wellspring of hungry tenderness inside her, eager and ready for the birth of her child. Her baby might not be planned but it was already very much loved.

The first few hours she was in hospital Billie was given gas and air to cope with the contractions but nothing seemed to be happening very fast. By noon the next day the contractions were coming closer together and were more painful. Billie was getting exhausted and it was at that point that the doctor realised that the baby was in a posterior position with its head stuck in her pelvis.

'You're carrying a big baby for a woman of your size and I don't think you can deliver without help. I believe the possibility of a C-section was discussed during your antenatal visits?' the doctor questioned, while the midwife urged Billie not to push any more.

Billie nodded anxious affirmation, too out of breath to speak.

Hilary gripped her hand. 'You'll be fine and so will the baby be—'

Everything moved very fast from that point. The procedure had to be explained to Billie and she had to sign consent papers before she was moved out of the labour room to the operating theatre. She was given an epidural and while her lower body went numb a little curtain was erected midway down her body so that she couldn't see anything. Time became a little blurred and there was a feeling of pressure and then suddenly Hilary was whooping with excitement.

'It's a boy, Billie!'

'A whopping great boy,' the doctor added.

The cry of a baby intervened and Billie's heart lurched. She was so eager to see him she could hardly contain herself while the staff took care of measuring him and making him presentable for his first meeting with his mum. He weighed ten pounds and he was very long, exactly what she might have expected with his father's genes; Alexei's family was one of tall, well-built men. At last her son was placed in her arms.

Tears stung Billie's eyes as she looked down into that adorable little face and carefully tracked her gaze over his big dark eyes and the shock of black hair that proclaimed his paternity. 'He's…gorgeous,' she whispered chokily, smoothing a wondering fingertip over his baby-soft cheek.

At that moment everything she had undergone to have him seemed worthwhile. In the early stages of her pregnancy, Hilary had talked her through every option from termination to adoption, yet nobody loved babies more than Hilary, who had never had the opportunity to have one of her own.

'Any idea what you'll call him?' her aunt prompted, stepping back to let the nurse reclaim the baby, for Billie's eyes were very definitely sliding shut.

'Nik—'

'What?' Hilary queried.

'Nikolos.' Billie spelled out the letters through lips that barely moved.

'Isn't giving him a Greek name a little revealing?'

'I've lived in Greece since I was eight,' her niece reminded her, and on that thought she drifted asleep while her mind swept her back seventeen years to her very first meeting with Alexei Nikolos Drakos…

The boys shouted rude words at Bliss when she followed them onto the beach. She knew the words were wrong but she didn't understand their meaning and refused to let their attitude bother her. At least the boys talked to her in some way, recognising her actual existence. The girls in the village school, on the other hand, shunned her, whispering behind her back and shooting disapproving looks at her while excluding her from their games and conversations. It was very similar to the way her mother was treated by the local women. After a year, Bliss had discovered that life on the Greek island of Speros could be very lonely for a little girl who didn't fit in.

Bliss hated everything about herself: her lack of height, her fiery red head of hair and skinny body, even her pale skin, which burned horribly in the sun. The fact she had no father meant yet more mortification on an island where single parents were frowned upon. And although Bliss would never have admitted it to anyone in those days, her mother embarrassed her most of all.

As Lauren often reminded her daughter, she was only thirty years old and couldn't be expected to live as if she were a 'dried-up old hag'. An artist, Lauren rented a small house in the village and sold watercolours to the well-off tourists who patronised the exclusive resort spa at the other end of the island. None of the local women dressed as her mother did. Lauren was most often to be found clad in skimpy bikini bottoms with her full braless breasts bouncing in a cut-off T-shirt. Bliss believed that her mother, with her lovely long blonde hair, jewelled tummy button and endless tanned legs, was very beautiful, but she was beginning to think that only men liked that fact, for Lauren only ever had male friends.

That particular day, Alexei had come off one of the fishing boats being dragged up the sand so she hadn't known who he was at first. He was a tall, rangy boy in his early teens, and she initially mistook him for an adult when he frowned in her direction and waded in among the jeering boys and demanded to know what was going on. Silence fell, the same sort of silence that the village priest could command. Shame-faced glances were exchanged and Alexei asked her name. One of the boys supplied it with a suggestive laugh and a gesture that set all the boys off again.

'Bliss,' Alexei repeated deadpan, strolling over to her. 'You're the little English girl. Bliss is a stupid name. I would call you Billie—'

'That's a boy's name,' she argued.

'It suits you better,' he told her with a shrug, lazy dark golden eyes resting on her with only the most fleeting interest before he turned away to address one of the older boys in the group, Damon Marios, the doctor's son, and said something to him in Greek too fast for her to follow as she was still learning the language. Damon flushed and kicked the sand.

'Who is he?' she asked Damon when Alexei had climbed into the car waiting for him at the harbour and was driven off.

'Alexei Drakos.'

And that was all he had to say to her even then for her to understand. The Drakos family lived in feudal splendour in a huge villa overlooking a beautiful bay at the quiet end of the island. For more than a hundred years the Drakos family had owned the island and they also owned the resort, the businesses and most of the houses in the village. The family controlled everything that related to Speros from the planning laws to who lived and worked on the island. Speros was the Drakos fiefdom and it was ruled with a rod of iron. The locals, however, were perfectly happy with that state of affairs because there were well-paid jobs at the resort and the village businesses opening up only added to their prosperity. Alexei's father had also built a new school and a small hospital and, at a time when other islands were losing their young people to the mainland, the population on Speros was steadily increasing.

'Mum, is the Drakos family very rich?' she asked when her mother was cooking a meal that evening, a rare event as Billie was often left to fend for herself when it came to food and generally lived on sandwiches and fruit.

'They're loaded,' Lauren volunteered with a grimace. 'But they don't impress me at all. They're not one whit better than we are, for all their cash. The old man, Constantine, was married three times and he never managed to have any children. Then his Russian mistress, Natasha—who's half his age—fell pregnant with Alexei, his only child. Constantine divorced his third wife and married Natasha two days before she gave birth to Alexei—'

'What's a mistress?' Billie asked her mother.

'You'd never understand,' Lauren replied, already tiring of the subject.

School became a little less unbearable for her after that night. Everyone started calling her Billie. The boys stopped teasing her and Damon's sister, Marika, spoke to her in passing. But nobody was ever allowed to come and play at her house and she was never invited into anyone else's home. Her mother's boyfriends came in a continual stream from the resort where Lauren often made extra money working as a waitress. Usually backpackers, some only stayed for a night or two, while others ended up living with Lauren and her daughter for weeks on end. By the time she was eleven years old, Billie, who had abandoned her birth name entirely to avoid the sniggers it invited, understood that it was Lauren's free and easy lifestyle with her lovers that scandalised the locals and that had led to her own exclusion from island life. Other mothers were afraid that she would grow up to live like Lauren and act as a bad influence on their daughters.

Two days after her eleventh birthday, Billie met Alexei Drakos for the second time. She was out exploring when a sudden thunderstorm sent her running along the harbour road for the shelter of home. Alexei stopped his beach buggy to give her a lift and insisted on going right to the door with her.

'Where's your mother?' he asked, scanning the empty silent little house.

'In Athens,' she told him innocently. 'She got the ferry on Friday—'

'That's four days ago,' Alexei incised harshly. 'Where is she staying in Athens?'

'She has friends there.'

'Do you have their name or phone number?' Alexei pressed while the thunder boomed out in loud cracks beyond the house walls and made her pale and flinch.

'No. Why would I need it?' she asked. 'There's nothing wrong. I can manage fine on my own.'

'When will she be back?'

'She said this Friday.'

With a bitten-off exclamation, Alexei strode across the room to the refrigerator and flung the door open to study the bare shelves within. 'What are you eating?'

'There are tins in the cupboard,' she answered stiffly, feeling threatened by his mood and his behaviour. 'Not that it's any of your business.'

'You will have to come home with me.'

'No, of course I won't—why would I? I'm perfectly happy here in my own home,' she protested.

And Alexei being Alexei, and having no patience whatsoever, simply lifted her off her feet and dropped her back in the buggy before speeding back to his home. Ignoring her protests, he dragged her inside and explained the situation to his parents in rapid Greek. His father shrugged and went back into his office, complaining at the interruption. His glamorous mother studied Billie as if she were something the cat had brought in and had asked if there were any neighbours prepared to help out. As assured and decisive as any adult, even at the age of sixteen, Alexei handed Billie over to the housekeeper and she spent that night and the two that followed housed in staff accommodation. There she was well fed and well looked after for the first time in more years than she could recall. Lauren had always lacked the maternal gene. Before that day only Billie's aunt, Hilary, had ever paid that much heed to the little girl's comfort.

Of course, had she been a more normal girl perhaps she would have formed a crush on Alexei as she grew up. After all, he was the island pin-up, worshipped by every girl between ten and twenty-five on Speros. From his film-star looks to his growing bad-boy reputation and the sexual exploits diligently reported by the gossip magazines, Alexei made headlines almost from the moment he hit puberty and followed faithfully in the lusty footsteps of his father and his grandfather. But after the terrible row Billie had with her mother because she'd admitted to others that she'd been left alone for a week, and a subsequent, very embarrassing visit from the island priest, who had been tasked with the challenge of telling Lauren that leaving her daughter for so long was unacceptable, Billie's main impression of Alexei was of a frighteningly dominant and interfering personality who did exactly as he liked at all times, regardless of the damage he might do to anyone else.

While Billie boarded in Athens during the week and attended secondary school, it was Damon Marios she fell for while they travelled back and forth on the ferries at weekends, he to his private school, she to her far less fancy state institution. By then she was seventeen years old and, for quite a few weeks, believed her feelings were reciprocated for she and Damon met secretly for coffee, going for walks, talking a mile-a-minute to each other and discovering similar interests.

Of course, she should have known better than to believe that dreams came true or that she could ever be seen as anything other than shameless Lauren's illegitimate daughter, a murky step below the other girls on the island. She still remembered the cold hard fear that gripped her one evening at the ferry terminal when

Damon suddenly dropped her hand and turned away
from her. Looking up, she saw Alexei strolling towards
them. Already a qualified pilot, Alexei had had to ditch
his plane in the sea the previous month and the shock
of his son's near-death experience had traumatised his
father, who had grounded him. Now in his last year at
university, Alexei was very much an adult. For the rest
of the journey, Damon ignored Billie as studiously as if
she had been a stranger.

'I'll drop you off,' Alexei declared at the harbour while
Damon hurried off homeward with a down-bent head.

'I don't need a lift.' Sixth sense warned her and she
didn't want to get into the sports car but she did anyway.

'Don't be stupid,' Alexei said drily. 'I'm only trying
to protect you from making a big mistake. Your mother
won't bother.'

'I don't know what you're talking about—'

'Damon, the leading light of the Marios family. He'll
screw you but he'll never take you seriously or take you
home with him. Didn't you get that message today when
he acted like he didn't know you around me?'

Like a knife cutting through tender flesh, his blunt
forecast tore through Billie and she looked back at him,
focusing on the lean bronzed beauty of his features with
furious condemnation. 'You don't know him!'

'I know Damon very well. His family will never accept
you and he hasn't got the backbone to fight for you. He's
a *nice* guy but he does as he's told. Cut your losses and
ditch him now before you get in any deeper—'

'I don't want your advice!' she shrieked at him in
Greek.

'Suit yourself,' Alexei drawled silkily. 'But whatever you do, keep your knickers on. All Greek men fantasise about having a virgin in the marriage bed.'

'That is a disgusting thing to say!' Billie launched back at him in a positive rage. 'I love Damon—'

'You're seventeen. You're not old enough to love anyone,' Alexei derided, stopping outside her house and leaning across her to throw open the door as if he couldn't wait to be rid of her. The male scent of his skin tinged by some expensive cologne wafted across her. She froze, rigid at that first taste of intimacy with a man, a fleeting intimacy that had the miraculous power to make her body prickle all over with uneasy awareness. That response shook her up because she had never reacted that way to Damon.

'I don't think I've ever disliked anyone quite so much,' Billie snapped in as cold and controlled a voice as she could manage.

'I'm always knee deep in women who are crazy about me,' Alexei countered with amusement. 'I doubt if I'll notice the absence of one little girl from my hordes of fans—'

'You're so incredibly bigheaded!' Billie flung, stepping out of the car in one electrified movement of rejection, her cheeks still burning hotly from that crack about keeping her underwear on.

A shockingly charismatic smile slanted across Alexei's wide sensual mouth and his stunning dark golden eyes gleamed. 'But still much more of a man than Damon will ever be…'

CHAPTER TWO

A YEAR later, Billie finished school and fought her mother hard for the freedom to go to university to study for a business degree. To survive, she had to work endless hours in a student bar where, mercifully, the low pay was matched with free meals. Aged twenty-one, she took her first job in a small import firm in Piraeus where, no matter how hard she worked, her male colleagues got the recognition and she got all the routine administrative tasks. When she saw Drakos Industries advertising a well-paid PA post on the Internet the following year, she wasted no time in applying.

Alexei Drakos had quickly tired of working for his billionaire father in the family shipping line. Breaking away, he had set up Drakos Industries at the age of twenty four, had made millions and was already well on the way to becoming a formidable tycoon in his own right. 'The Shark,' *Time* magazine had labelled him in an article marvelling at the speed with which he'd shaken off his reputation as a jet set playboy to demonstrate his worth as a shrewd entrepreneur.

As part of the application process for the job, Billie was one of the lucky few allotted a place in a day-long assessment. It was a gruelling experience comprised of working against the clock and handling difficult personalities but, forty-eight hours later, she learned that she had passed this first stage and had won an interview with Alexei. She was surprised he took so active a part in recruitment.

By the time she walked into his big fancy office in Athens clad in her smartest clothes, she was high on nerves. Sleek as a jungle predator in his black designer suit, Alexei surveyed her. 'I was surprised to see your name on the shortlist.'

Billie looked steadily back at him, noting the toughness that time had added to his lean strong face. 'I just want someone to give me a chance to do a proper job where I can use my brain—'

'And you think I might?' His brilliant dark eyes were nailed to her, his wide sensual mouth cool, discouraging.

'I don't think you will mark me down because I was born in England—'

'A positive panoply of praise from someone who doesn't like me,' Alexei mocked lazily. 'But you're right. I don't care where you came from, I'm only interested in who you are now. What could you offer me as an employee?'

'I'm very discreet and I work fast and hard. I also have good ideas—'

'Everyone's got ideas. I don't always want to hear them…'

'I'm a great organiser and I can think on my feet.'

Alexei rested his unsettling gaze on her and she

shifted uneasily, suddenly alarmingly conscious of her every physical flaw. It was as though his very masculine perfection highlighted her deficiencies. Her vibrant mane of hair was restrained in a French plait, her green eyes bright against her pale skin. Full as she was at breast and hip, she felt she lacked the height to successfully carry off her curves. Her waist was small though and her legs slim. Lauren had always refused to tell her daughter who her father was and Billie had wondered cynically if her mother even knew. Certainly, she had signally failed to inherit any of her mother's leggy blonde assets.

'The position on offer would entail working directly for me.'

Belatedly, Billie understood why she was receiving an interview from the boss himself. 'I'd like to know exactly what the job is.'

'The successful candidate will take care of everything I don't have time for. He or she will often travel with me and the hours will be long. The job will cover everything from setting up appointments with my tailor to buying gifts on my behalf and barring women I don't want to see or hear from any more,' Alexei spelt out bluntly. 'It is a post which demands considerable trust on my part. A confidentiality agreement will be included in the contract of employment, making it illegal to share any revelations about me or my lifestyle with the press.'

In truth, Billie was totally taken aback by the extent of what was being offered to her. Even if it didn't sound like her role would have much of a business angle to it, any position working directly for Alexei would still add kudos to her CV.

'I want to hire someone willing to turn their hand to anything I ask at any time of day—'

'A slave?' Billie quipped and then wished she could bite off her facetious tongue when his superb bone structure tensed and cooled.

'A very well-paid one. I don't work by the clock. Neither do I want someone who counts the hours or excludes certain tasks.'

Billie nodded, tantalised by the prospect of travelling and reasoning that she was free as a bird and well able to cope with such a demanding role. The following week, she was informed that she had got the job. The salary took her breath away being, even at a conservative estimate, twice what she had expected. On her first day she arrived neatly attired in her newest suit.

'You need to smarten up your work wardrobe,' Alexei informed her at the first glimpse he had of her. Seemingly impervious to the flush of mortification warming her face, he handed her a business card. 'And this first time, you can do it at my expense—'

Billie stiffened. 'That's not necessary—'

'Look in the mirror. You are a frump,' Alexei countered bluntly, 'and I always decide what's necessary.'

Feeling cut off at the knees, Billie took the card and went that same afternoon to an upmarket store, where she was kitted out with the sort of figure-hugging clothing and high heels that she had always deemed unsuitable in a working environment. On the third day she wore a skirt well above her knees that outlined the curve of her hips and a jacket that nipped in at her waist, accentuating the shape and size of her breasts. She didn't like her reflection; she thought it was unprofessional.

'Turn round,' Alexei instructed casually during his morning coffee break and he studied her with assessing cool, oblivious to her blushing discomfiture. 'That's a major improvement.'

'I prefer a more formal look,' she told him starchily.

Dark golden eyes alight with amusement as he absorbed her rigid stance and tight mouth, Alexei laughed out loud. 'You're young and pretty. Make the most of it while you can.'

As Billie looked at his vibrantly handsome features she felt the sensual buzz of his compelling attraction right down to the centre of her bones and it unnerved her, for she did not want to feel that way around her boss. But even though she fought it, she was flattered by the simple fact that this man, who kept company with some of the world's most beautiful women, could deem her 'pretty'. Suddenly the high heels and the short skirt no longer felt like such a bad idea.

Alexei's business team was all male and she was assiduously ignored until the first time Alexei phoned her in the middle of the night to help him handle a minor crisis and the team then discovered that they had to liaise with Alexei through her. Later that week, with the ice broken, she took the opportunity to ask one of the men why she was excluded to such an extent.

Panos gave her an uneasy glance. 'Sooner or later the female staff on the team end up in bed with Alexei,' he told her reluctantly. 'And that makes us all uncomfortable. After a week or so, Alexei always transfers that person out of the main office to another job. We know the score. Four women have already come and gone in your particular role in a short time.'

Billie managed a calm smile. 'It's not going to happen that way with me. I'm here for the long haul.'

But that warning also put her on her guard around Alexei, even though she soon appreciated that the fault was rarely his. A phenomenal number of women, exposed to Alexei's charismatic good looks and wealth, literally threw themselves at him the first opportunity they got. His sex life frequently shocked her, for the very nature of her job and her need to work closely to him meant that she saw virtually every woman he had in his life. During the second month after employing her, he spent the night on his yacht with twin blonde models, Katia and Kerry, who could barely string an intelligent sentence between them.

'Take them out shopping,' Alexei instructed Billie the next morning, tossing her a credit card. 'And don't look at the price tags. I'm not on a budget.'

Billie travelled to shore in the launch with the two giggling blondes, who seemed not to have a care in the world. Indeed, acting as Alexei's entertainment for one night only appeared to have energised their spirits. While she escorted the twins round the exclusive boutiques on shore, she was forced to listen to a great deal of sexual banter about what Alexei was like in bed. Her every attempt to change the subject was turned aside and by the time she thankfully parted from his effervescent lovers she was very angry and determined never to have to repeat the experience. She wasted no time in tackling the subject when she found Alexei out on deck on her return to *Sea Queen*.

'Please don't put me in a position again where I have to escort your lady friends around while they discuss your sexual performance during the night before,' Billie framed in a tone of tremulous rage, her green eyes as bright as emeralds, her face pink and set in censorious lines.

Alexei dealt her a startled glance and then burst out laughing, astonishing her with his reaction almost as much as she had astonished him with her verbal attack. 'How did I rate? Did I figure as a hero or a zero?'

'That is not something I would wish to discuss with my employer,' Billie assured him thinly, rigidly un-amused by his attitude for he was refusing to take her objection seriously.

'You're a real prude.' Alexei lounged back against the rail, a darkly handsome and graceful presence in a light-weight beige summer suit. 'I'm surprised. We both have liberal parents in that regard and yet the experience seems to have affected us very differently. A good time was had by all and sex was not a serious subject when I was growing up. I prefer to keep it that way now—'

'I'm not a prude,' Billie proclaimed sharply, her voice rising a little because she was deeply embarrassed by his reference to her mother's promiscuous lifestyle. That was part of the past she had left behind her and she very much resented any reminder of it.

'Billie…the sight of me having breakfast with two women this morning offended you,' Alexei countered drily. 'But you are not required to exercise your moral

convictions while you work for me. I'm not interested
in what you think. My private life is just that—*mine*. My
sole expectation of you is that you do your job—'

Her slim shoulders straight as a ruler, growing tension bubbling through her small frame, Billie breathed,
'And I've told you that I have limits. This morning,
Katia and Kerry crossed them. I was embarrassed to be
out in public with them. They dress, behave and talk like
hookers—'

'I don't sleep with hookers,' Alexei cut in, his rich
dark drawl harsh in reproof. 'One more suggestion
along those lines and you're fired.'

Outraged by his attitude and white hot with resentment, Billie snapped, 'Because I've got standards?
Because I expect to be treated like a professional during
my working day?'

'You don't have standards, you have a narrow mind.
I warned you before I hired you that I would expect you
to cope with everything I throw at you—'

Determined not to be intimidated by the anger in his
scorching dark golden eyes, Billie lifted her chin. 'Katia
and Kerry were a step too far—'

'If I can't count on you to follow orders, you're no
use to me. I will not tolerate any member of my staff
telling me what I can and can't do, or complaining about
the responsibilities I give them,' Alexei delivered coldly.
'So, if that is how it is, clear your desk and I'll have you
flown back to Athens.'

Billie had gone too far to back down and, her head
held high, she went indoors to pack her belongings.
How dared Alexei Drakos christen her a prude? Just

because he slept around and looked for nothing more than beauty and sex from his partners!

Lauren's habit of bedding every man she met had made Billie very cautious in her dealings with the opposite sex. How could she not have been influenced by the distaste and contempt that Lauren's lifestyle had roused in so many people? In every way possible Billie drew a clear boundary line between her life and her mother's. She never wore revealing clothes. She didn't flirt with other women's men. Casual uncommitted sex was anathema to her. She'd only ever had three relationships—Damon, and two at university that had come to nothing after her boyfriends sought easier conquests. A highly sexed and very handsome philanderer like Alexei Drakos was Billie's worst nightmare in the partnership stakes.

Billie returned via Athens to the island of Speros, where Lauren soon dragged the story of her dismissal out of her daughter.

'Why didn't you just laugh at those women? Why do you take everything so seriously?' Lauren demanded, her incomprehension patent. 'You're your own worst enemy—you land the job of a lifetime and straight away you screw it up!'

'I don't need this, Mum,' Billie breathed tautly. 'But don't worry. I can still cover your rent for the next couple of months and by then I should have found another job.'

'You certainly won't find one as well paid. What got into you?' Lauren snapped. 'Alexei Drakos is a young, good-looking single guy and all he is doing is what comes naturally. Of course he doesn't want to be tied down at his age or with his opportunities. What does it have to do with you?'

'I just don't like his lifestyle or his attitudes and I'm with him so much I can't avoid either.'

Lauren dealt her smaller daughter a scornful look. 'You've got the hots for him and you're jealous—'

'No, I haven't!' Billie argued, incensed and shaken by that accusation.

'He's gorgeous. *I* wouldn't say no,' Lauren replied with a voluptuous pout and a toss of her blonde head.

Billie resisted a shrewish urge to agree that no wasn't a word that came easily to her mother's lips. In her forties, Lauren was no longer the siren she had once been and there were fewer men in her life. Eighteen months had passed since Billie had last come home to find that she was sharing her mother's house with a resident toy boy. But the very suggestion of Alexei and Lauren together made her feel physically sick and this knowledge worked on her that night while she tossed and turned and failed to find restful sleep.

Was she attracted to Alexei more than she was prepared to admit? Had she been mortally offended by Katia and Kerry because they had shared Alexei's bed? Was that because in some dim dark corner of her mind she was jealous of the carefree and sexually confident twins? She shuddered at the suspicion. Alexei was as bronzed, beautiful and flawless in feature and physique as a Greek god and she was a flesh and blood ordinary woman who could hardly be impervious to that reality. But being aware that he was a very good looking guy did not mean that she was physically attracted to him, did it? And even if it did, what did it matter? Nothing was ever likely to come of the fact. Alexei only went for gorgeous women and she was much too sensible to be tempted even if he should have a weak moment in her radius. Mortified by her growing suspicion that she might not be as unprejudiced or as principled as she had fondly believed, Billie lay awake until dawn.

The following day, she returned to Athens and the apartment she shared with two other women. She needed to be on the spot to job-hunt. She put her short-lived job with Alexei into a mental box and hammered it shut, but she soon discovered that the very brevity of her employment with him had harmed her standing in the eyes of others. A month later, she was less angry with Alexei and angrier with herself for damaging her career prospects. By then her proud and impulsive walkout on a matter of principle was beginning to strike her as more foolish than brave.

That was the mood she was in when the doorbell went one evening and she answered it to find one of Alexei's security team facing her. 'Mr Drakos would like to speak to you. I have a car waiting outside for you,' he volunteered before swinging away and heading downstairs, it not even crossing his mind that she might dare to refuse such an invitation.

Billie stepped back into the apartment, glancing at herself in the hall mirror. Her hair, freshly washed, lay in vibrant waves across her shoulders. She was wearing cropped jeans, a sleeveless cotton top and canvas pumps. She lifted her chin. What did Alexei want? She could just say no to the offer of a meeting and then she would burn with curiosity ever after, she completed ruefully. He could just want to see her about something she had dealt with while she still worked for him. Grabbing her bag, she slammed the door behind her.

Alexei had a ritzy apartment in Athens, just one of the many properties scattered round the world that he owned, since he had already inherited several from his father's side of the family. She recalled his town house in Venice, a chateau in the south of France, a house in New York, a ski lodge in Switzerland and a ranch in Australia. Taking care of those properties and their staff had been her responsibility and she had been looking forward to visiting each and every one of them at some stage.

Alexei was on the phone chattering in French when she was shown into a massive living area with bold designer furniture and an array of modern art and sculpture. A wide-shouldered, lean-hipped figure clad in linen trousers and an open shirt, Alexei was barefoot and clearly fresh out of the shower. His black hair was still spiky and shiny with moisture, his aggressive jawline rough with the shadow of blue-black stubble that accentuated the wide sensual allure of his masculine mouth.

Just looking at him, she felt his impact like a thud in her ears and a kick in her stomach. He was all rogue male, from his dark-as-midnight eyes heavily fringed by lashes to the slice of torso visible between the unbuttoned edges of his shirt, which revealed a matt of dark curls sprinkled across his bronzed chest and the six-pack stomach that Katia and Kerry had raved about…among other things. Her mouth dry and feeling oddly breathless, Billie squashed those inappropriate thoughts—but not in time to stop her disobedient gaze dropping to the distinctive masculine bulge at his crotch.

Reddening to the roots of her hair as fully as only a woman of her complexion could, Billie yanked her eyes upward and said jerkily, 'You wanted to see me?'

He shifted a hand, which urged her to wait until he had finished his phone call and, that fast, she wanted to shout at him again. Her spine stiffened, her full soft mouth compressing, for he had summoned her like a minion across the city at seven in the evening and he was still putting his own wishes first. And it would always be like that, she acknowledged tautly. He was poised there, more beautiful than any mortal male had any right to be, and the world was his oyster because he was a blue-blooded filthy-rich Drakos. In *his* life, people always dropped everything to run and do his bidding. It had been that way for him since he was born.

Constantine Drakos had truly idolised his one and only child. Every cough and sniffle Alexei had suffered had been a major episode for his father. Alexei had had a bodyguard before he could even walk. A weaker child would have been indelibly scarred by such a protected upbringing but Constantine had found that he had a fight on his hands as Alexei had fought his ultra-safe regime every step of the way. He had taken part in dangerous sports at school; he had gone out fishing on the elderly boats of the village fleet; he had learned to sail alone; he had even learned to fly. Full of restive boundless energy, he had always challenged himself and those around him. He'd let nothing and nobody hold him back from what he wanted to be.

'Sorry about that.' Alexei sighed, tossing aside the phone. 'Take a seat.'

Billie sank down onto the sofa behind her, closed her hands together neatly on her lap and sent him an enquiring look.

'I've tried out two personal assistants since you left and rejected both. They couldn't handle your job—'

'At the end I couldn't handle it either,' she pointed out, and then wondered why she was drawing that failing to his attention again.

'It is important to me that I don't have to deal with all the hassle of being a Drakos—the properties, the social invitations, my relatives. I need to concentrate on business,' he breathed impatiently. 'When I'm not working, I like a smooth peaceful life. For the six weeks that you were in charge I enjoyed perfect peace. I want you to come back and work for me again.'

Billie was tense: she was flattered and troubled at one and the same time. 'I'm not sure that would be a good idea—we didn't gel.'

'From my point of view, I barely noticed you were around most of the time,' Alexei volunteered. 'You're very quiet.'

Not best pleased to hear that she was just part of the wallpaper as far as he was concerned, Billie met his stunning dark eyes unwarily and her tummy performed a somersault. 'I assumed that that was what you would want.'

'Why are you always so tense?' Alexei demanded with a sudden frown. 'You were like that around me even when you were a kid. Look at you now—sitting there as frozen as if you're waiting to be tipped into a pool of hungry sharks!'

In a defensive move, Billie folded her arms. 'I never know what you're going to do or say next. It's…unnerving.'

'You could learn to live with it. If you start back to work tomorrow, I'll double your salary,' Alexei murmured silkily, watching the sunshine play across the gold and copper shades in her auburn hair, which was much longer than he had appreciated and surprisingly attractive. He went for blondes, not for redheads, but for the first time ever he could see the draw of her striking colouring, particularly in the contrast between her hair and her pale, flawless skin.

'But I haven't even said I'll come back yet and offering to double my salary is just crazy and extravagant!'

His expressive mouth took on a humorous quirk. 'I can afford to be. If having to occasionally deal with the women in my life is a sticking point, you can hire an assistant to deal with them on your behalf. I don't care.'

It was a compliment to her efficiency that he should be so keen to have her working for him again. As he smiled that lazy smile and remained poised there in the sunshine pouring through the windows she was, for the first time, hugely conscious of his compelling charm. He was offering her an amazing salary to do a job she enjoyed. With that amount of money coming in, she would no longer need to worry about Lauren falling behind with the rent or not being able to buy her own property.

'All right,' Billie said gruffly. 'I'll start back tomorrow.'

'You didn't get another job, did you?'

'I couldn't come up with a good enough excuse for leaving your employ after only six weeks!' Billie responded with spirit.

Alexei laughed. 'Where were your wits? You should've said I made a pass at you. With my reputation everyone would have believed it.'

Billie turned a slow hot pink and evaded his keen gaze. 'That idea never occurred to me.'

Probably because it would never have occurred to her either that anyone would *believe* she had actually found his attentions unwelcome and turned him down, Billie acknowledged ruefully...

CHAPTER THREE

'THAT should wrap it up,' Alexei pronounced, stabbing a final button on the keyboard before pushing away his laptop in a rare gesture of rejection. Rising up, he stretched like a lion, flexing strong muscles bunched up by the constraint of sitting at a desk before shrugging back his sleeve to check the slender gold Rolex on his wrist. It was after one in the morning. 'You should have told me how late it was.'

Blinking, Billie stifled a yawn. 'I *did*.'

That quiet rejoinder made his handsome mouth quirk. Billie was the only employee who ever answered him back. He studied her with narrowed eyes, taking in the white sleeveless top she wore and the full rounded thrust of her breasts against the fine cotton that was pulling at the pearl buttons. More than a lush handful, he calculated, pressure building at his groin as he instinctively pictured the baring of her firm pink-tipped flesh. He was startled by his reaction. Evidently, it had been too long since he had been with a woman, he reflected in exasperation.

Even as he looked, Billie was reaching for the jacket she had removed. In the past two years during which Billie had been on his staff, she was always covered up, buttoned up, zipped up, just as her hair was always clipped, plaited or tied—everything held in tight restraint. In an age when other women were happy to reveal as much flesh as possible, Billie's modesty made her stand out from the crowd. Even when she went swimming she donned a modest black swimsuit that would not have shamed a nun. Yet the feminine mystique she was careful to preserve was strangely and powerfully sexy, Alexei acknowledged. Odd, too, how he felt guilty even thinking about her in such a way. But then he was almost certain that, rare as it would be, Billie was still a virgin.

'You'll have to stay here tonight. You can't disturb your mother this late,' he commented, lifting the house phone to issue instructions to the housekeeper, Anatalya.

'I'm sure it won't bother her if I wake her up,' Billie protested, uneasy at the prospect of spending the night at the Drakos villa where she generally felt like a peasant-born intruder.

'Don't make a fuss,' Alexei groaned in all-male irritation, silencing her.

Behind his back, Billie flushed at the reproof. The door opened, revealing not the maid she had expected, but Alexei's mother, Natasha.

'I'll show you upstairs,' the tall, still-beautiful brunette said with an artificial smile. Billie was never more conscious of her humble little-island-girl beginnings than she was in the radius of Alexei's glamorous and patronising mother.

Alexei said something in Russian to the older woman. Dark eyes warming only as they rested on her only child, Natasha left the room to escort Billie up the palatial staircase. 'Do you often work this late for my son?'

'Not that often. But I'm very well paid, Mrs Drakos. Occasional long hours go with the territory,' Billie pointed out.

A door was pressed open. Rather stiff and taut, Billie walked in. She was always aware that Alexei's mother didn't approve of her working for Alexei. She had no idea why, only the vague suspicion that Natasha didn't think Lauren Foster's daughter was good enough to work in so trusted a position.

Her reluctant hostess was already turning to leave when Billie noticed the man's shirt lying discarded on the carpet and put two and two together fast. 'Is this…Alexei's room?' she breathed in dismay.

'Why, yes, I assumed that…' Natasha Drakos gave a little suggestive shrug of her slim shoulders.

'You assumed wrong.' It was Alexei's assured drawl from behind the older woman that broke the tension and the brief, awkward silence that had fallen.

Billie's face was drenched with colour and she could barely bring herself to look at him or his parent. 'I really think I should go home—'

'I'm sorry,' Natasha Drakos murmured. 'I misunderstood.'

Rather than make more of a scene, Billie allowed herself to be shown into the room next door but she felt humiliated. She was well qualified and she performed her job to the highest standards, for no Drakos had yet been born capable of accepting shoddy work. Why did Alexei's mother have to assume that her role automatically extended to warming her son's bed? That was a very demeaning supposition. Locked in that thought, she was then nonplussed by the discovery that her hostess had yet to leave her alone.

'You probably think you're very clever getting so close to Alexei and worming your way into his confidence,' the older woman breathed with cold dark eyes, her angry hostility laid bare now that her son was no longer within hearing. 'But you're wasting your time. He's a Drakos and, although he'll think nothing of sleeping with you when there's not a more attractive prospect available, he'll never marry beneath him.'

Billie did momentarily toy with the idea of responding with the simple fact that Alexei's father had done exactly that when he chose to wed his pregnant mistress, a little-known fashion model from a poverty-stricken home in some obscure industrial town in Russia. But Billie had never been bitchy and she was reluctant to rattle Natasha's cage when she was an increasingly frequent visitor to the villa.

With that acid condemnation, Natasha mercifully departed and Billie exhaled. At least she now knew why Alexei's mother didn't like her. She thought Billie was too close to her son and in spite of Alexei's denial that he and his PA were intimate, Natasha remained unconvinced. Initially, Billie was vaguely amused to think she could figure as a clever, calculating gold-digger in Natasha's eyes, but she was not at all amused by the comment that Alexei would only sleep with her if she was the only woman available to slake his high-voltage libido.

How much more hurtful and wounding could one woman be to another? Billie wondered once she had got into the comfortable bed. She was already very much aware that she was not good looking. After all, she had grown up in the shadow of a handsome mother and Alexei's women were always noted beauties. Billie knew her best points and her worst ones. She was now also wondering if it had been a mistake not to date at least one of the men who had asked her out since she started working for Alexei. Perhaps if, at some stage, she had had a boyfriend Alexei's mother would not have regarded her with such poisonous suspicion.

Billie lay in the moonlit room and mulled over the awful truth that daily exposure to Alexei had made other men pale by comparison. Alexei had more sex appeal than any man she had ever met. Although she tried not to think about her employer on those terms, he was gorgeous to look at and usually very entertaining to be with, because he was clever, witty and dynamic while also being amazingly attuned to what women liked. Only Alexei would order her a hot chocolate topped with melted marshmallows at the end of a particularly long or difficult day, or send her for a relaxing hot stone massage when she got headaches at that certain time of the month. Times without number he'd picked up on things other men would have failed to notice.

Maybe, Billie began thinking anxiously, it was her own fault that Alexei's mother had thought it necessary to warn Billie off her son. Maybe her own behaviour was to blame for Natasha's belief that she shared Alexei's bed. Just at that moment it suddenly struck Billie that, for a mere employee, she was far too attached to Alexei. Somewhere down the line her protective barriers had crumbled. Alexei was brilliant in business and working for him was exciting. But she admired him too much, she conceded grudgingly. When once she had disapproved of his energetic sex life, now she turned her head away from the evidence of it, reasoning that his lovers were experienced women who knew the score. When had she started making excuses for his lifestyle?

Just when had she started falling in love with her boss?

Shattered by that belated glimpse into her innermost heart, Billie was furious that she could have been so blind to the feelings she was developing. More than a few of the women Alexei had had affairs with had descended into sobbing heartbreak in front of Billie when his interest had waned. Billie had offered tissues and platitudes in response, protecting Alexei from such aggravations, guarding his privacy as best she could. Why had it taken Natasha's taunts to make her appreciate that, over the past couple of years, she had got too close to the sun and got burned without even realising it? Was her attachment to Alexei equally obvious to others? Billie cringed, resolving that she needed a little space, time to get a grip on herself and her emotions again. She did not want to turn into one of those sad women who worked for the man they'd loved for years without ever being noticed by him, because being close to him was better than being without him entirely.

When she got up the next day, heavy-eyed from her

lack of sleep, it was to be greeted with the news that she had the day off because Alexei had gone out fishing with his father around dawn. One of the security guards gave her a lift to the village house she had bought for her mother six months earlier. The purchase had not been as straightforward as she had hoped, for at least one local had complained to the Drakos family about a foreigner like Billie being allowed to buy property on Speros and she had little doubt that allegations about Lauren's morals had also been part of the argument. Thankfully, Constantine Drakos had squashed the protests and approved the sale.

'My father believes that you and your mother have lived on the island long enough to be viewed as part of the community,' Alexei had told her.

'I'm grateful. I just want Lauren to have a secure home that no one can take away from her,' Billie had confided, not bothering to add that, from her point of view, buying a small house outright was cheaper and safer than trusting Lauren to use the money Billie gave her to pay the rent.

Lauren was delighted with her new home and had gone to unusual effort to furnish and decorate it.

Smiling at the window box of bright geraniums ornamenting the blue-painted front sill, Billie knocked on the rough-wood front door of the tumbledown whitewashed house at the end of a crumbling terrace. Her smile slid away a little when the door was opened by a strange man. Around thirty years old with long brown hair and an unshaven face that made him look more unkempt than trendy, he sported shorts and a T-shirt.

'You can only be Billie,' he said cheerfully. 'Lauren's in her studio.'

The tiny sunroom at the back of the house had become her mother's workplace. Her deeply tanned, leggy parent turned from her easel to say, 'When I saw the yacht had docked in the bay last night I expected you home.'

'I had to work late. If I'd known you were expecting me I'd have phoned.' Billie stretched up to dab a kiss on Lauren's cheek. 'Who's your guest?'

'Dean? He was a deckhand on a boat that called in a few weeks back. We met at the taverna and he decided he'd like to stay a while. I'm enjoying the company. You know how it is,' her mother told her, shooting a flirtatious glance at Dean, who was stationed in the doorway, denying Billie the privacy she would have preferred with her parent.

'I'll just go upstairs and change.' Billie came to a halt and had to say, 'Excuse me, Dean...' before her mother's boyfriend let her pass.

And, as Lauren had commented, Billie did indeed know how it was when it came to Lauren's boyfriends. They were usually backpackers, dropouts or seasonal workers, happy to latch onto the chance of free board and lodgings on an idyllic Greek island. Billie could not recall when her mother had last had a guest who contributed in any way to the household budget. But she was determined not to let Dean's presence spoil her brief stay.

Billie made a salad lunch for the three of them in the kitchen, coolly clad in a pair of shorts teamed with a tankini top. She glanced up while she was setting the

table and noticed that Dean was staring lasciviously at
her cleavage. A hot flush marking her cheeks, she looked
hurriedly away again. After they had eaten, she said she
was going down to the beach and went upstairs to put
on a T-shirt. When she came back down again Lauren
and Dean were whispering and kissing on the sofa and
she couldn't get out of the house quickly enough.

Not for the first time she wished she had her own
bolthole on Speros. If she moved out it would be yet
another nail in her mother's coffin as far as the locals
were concerned but after so many years did that really
matter? On the other hand, she had very little time off and
was usually staying on the yacht or in one of Alexei's
other properties when she was free. How much use would
she get out of an independent home on the island? It
would not be much of an investment either as privately
owned houses on the island had to be offered to the locals
first for sale, which kept prices artificially low.

That evening, they dined at the taverna—Billie's
treat, of course. By then she was noticing that her easy-
come-easy-go mother seemed unusually keen on Dean,
and that Dean drank too much and talked too loudly.
Billie was revolted by the way he kept on staring at her
breasts and the jokes he began to crack about busty
women. She went to bed early and stirred only when her
door opened some hours later.

'Mum?' she mumbled, drowsily trying to unclog her
lashes to open her eyes when the side of the bed gave
as someone came down on the mattress and tilted it.

The smell of beer and male sweat assailed her in
warning a split second before a bristly jaw line made

scratchy contact with her cheek. 'It's Dean,' her mother's boyfriend whispered thickly. 'Keep your voice down or you'll wake your ma, and we don't want to do that, do we?'

The instant he made physical contact her eyes flew wide in panic and her arms flailed wildly to push him away from her while her body frantically squirmed and heaved up to escape the weighty imprisonment of his body lying half over hers. 'Get off me! *Get out!*' she screamed at the top of her voice.

Within thirty seconds Lauren was in the room demanding to know why her boyfriend was falling off the end of her daughter's bed. Her mother had had a great deal to drink as well and the older woman lost no time in accusing Billie of trying to steal her man. In the midst of the resulting madness, in which her mother slapped her face hard, Billie got out of bed, gathered up her clothes, fought past Lauren's hysterical attempt to hold onto her and escaped into the bathroom to get dressed. By the time she emerged, her mother was shouting at her to get out of her house and never come back and the neighbours were banging on the party wall in complaint. Billie paused only long enough to grab up her bag, which she had not unpacked, and her phone.

Tearstained and trembling, she sat on a bollard down by the harbour, wondering what to do next. The sun was slowly rising in a crimson glow on the horizon. Nothing would make her go to the Drakos villa in such a state to ask for shelter, but *Sea Queen* was anchored out in the bay and she had no reservations about calling the yacht and asking for the launch to be sent out to pick her up.

The crew would think little of her request since she often went on board at odd hours without Alexei. The launch came quickly and she climbed in, her heart thudding fast as the boat drew closer to the giant white yacht that towered above them like a skyscraper. She was embarrassed when she realised that Captain McGregor had got out of bed to greet her. She thought he looked at her a little suspiciously and, after apologising for interrupting his sleep, took her leave of him as soon as she could.

Still shell-shocked by her ordeal at Dean and Lauren's hands, Billie felt dizzy and she kicked off her shoes and lay down on the bed in the opulent cabin Alexei had long since assigned to her in the guest—rather than in the crew—quarters. Her head was aching, her face was sore where she had been slapped and her hands were shaking so badly she had to set down the glass of water she was trying to drink. How could her mother have believed that she might welcome her boy-friend into her bed?

A loud rata-tat-tat on the door made her sit up with a start against the headboard. 'Come in!' she called with a frown; even that movement of her face hurt.

She was shocked when Alexei strode through the door looking rather less elegant and laid-back than was his wont. His black hair was tousled, he needed a shave and he was wearing jeans and a half-buttoned white dress shirt below a dinner jacket.

'What are you doing on board?' Billie burst out.

'McGregor phoned me.' His probing gaze a clear hot gold, Alexei came down on the bed on his knees beside her, suddenly, disturbingly close. But where Dean had brought her out in a cold sweat of fear and disgust, Alexei sent her heart racing in an all-out sprint.

'Why did the Captain phone you?' Billie dragged in a feverish breath, a bubble of heat bursting low in her tummy when she collided with his level golden gaze.

'My goodness, I'm so sorry you were disturbed, Alexei. I seem to be causing an awful lot of trouble, but I only needed a bed for the night and I couldn't face your mother. I'm sure she would've thought I was being cheeky turning up at the villa,' Billie gabbled, embarrassed and scarcely knowing what she was saying

His brilliant scrutiny oddly intent, Alexei lifted a bronzed long-fingered hand to turn her face into the pool of light shed by the lamp. His sleek ebony brows pleated and a stifled Greek curse escaped his taut mouth. 'McGregor phoned me because he could see that you had been attacked and naturally he was concerned.'

'*Attacked?*' she echoed in consternation.

'You have a long scratch and blood on your cheekbone and I suspect you may have a black eye by morning,' Alexei enumerated in curt explanation. 'Have you any other injuries?'

Billie lifted a tremulous hand and let the pads of her fingers brush the swelling soreness of her cheekbone. She had not even looked in a mirror since boarding. 'No. I'm perfectly fine.'

'You'd tell me that if you were lying here dying!' Alexei vented, unimpressed by that assurance. 'What happened? Who did this to you? Get over the idea that it's not done to admit to being hurt!'

'I really appreciate your concern but I'd prefer not to talk about it,' Billie mumbled, her eyes stinging like mad beneath her lowered lashes, because his concern on her behalf was more than she could bear while the thought of sharing such a kitchen-sink family drama with him just made her want to cringe in humiliation.

'Save the nonsense for fools. *Talk*,' Alexei instructed in an emphatic growl of threat that ratcheted up her tension and widened her gaze to focus on the harsh set of his darkly handsome features.

'Storm in a teacup,' she said shakily. 'Mum's boy-friend made a pass at me. He'd been drinking and he came into my room and lay down on my bed while I was sleeping—'

'He…did…*what*?' Alexei roared, springing back upright and glowering down at her in angry disbelief. 'You could have been raped!'

'But I wasn't. He gave me such a fright I screamed at him, and that woke Lauren up and she stormed in and misread the situation…' Billie was becoming too uncomfortable to hold his gaze. 'She slapped me—'

'Blamed you as well, no doubt,' Alexei incised with a gritty lack of hesitation. 'Why on earth did you waste your money buying her a house?'

'She's my mother and I know she's not perfect, but she's the only one I'll ever have,' Billie proffered, tight-mouthed.

'She's no mother at all when there's a man in the equation,' Alexei derided. 'If you had been more aware of your own interests you would have bought that house for your own use. You shouldn't be under the same roof as her.'

After Lauren's attack and abuse, Billie wondered if she ever would be under the same roof again. That violent response from her mother had gouged a big hole in Billie's heart. She knew alcohol had probably had a lot to do with her mother losing her head but it still hurt that Lauren could trust a man she had only met a few weeks ago more than she trusted her daughter.

'Well, it's too late now,' she muttered ruefully.

His attention still nailed to her swollen face and reddened eyes, Alexei breathed grimly. 'We'll see.'

Another knock sounded on the door and Alexei opened it to reveal the familiar, careworn face of the island doctor. The older man was taken aback by the state of Billie's face and, with all the assurance of someone who had known her as a child, he told her not to be silly when she insisted that an examination was unnecessary. He checked her eye and a steward brought a cold pack to help reduce the swelling. The doctor's probing revealed no further injury and the cut was minor enough to require no further attention.

'Now go to sleep,' Alexei instructed, leaving the cabin in the older man's company as soon as Billie had swallowed the painkillers she had been given. 'We'll talk tomorrow.'

Billie could not think what they could possibly have left to discuss. She lay curled up in the bed, tears seeping from below her lowered eyelids and stinging her sore face. She heard the doctor leave on the launch and its return when the sun was high in the sky because sleep had evaded her once again. A cup of tea was brought to her and she peered at her reflection in the mirror in horror: she looked a sight with one eye half shut by purple bruising and swelling that had destroyed the symmetry of her face. The phone by her bed buzzed.

Sunglasses firmly attached to her nose, she went up to the main deck to join Alexei for breakfast. He was on the phone and, sketching a movement with an imperious brown hand, he indicated that she go ahead and eat without waiting for him to join her. There were a couple of faces at the windows of his office and she reddened, knowing that the breakfast invite would be viewed as a sign of favouritism by the rest of the team, while anxiously wondering if word of her sudden arrival on board the yacht in the middle of the night had spread among the crew.

Alexei's dark rich masculine drawl took on the subtle change that warned her that he was talking to a woman. In Spanish? She had learned to recognise a number of the languages he spoke even if she couldn't speak them herself. He could well be talking to the actress, Lola Rodriquez, whom he had recently met in London. It was none of her business, Billie told herself urgently, squashing the beginnings of an envious daydream in which she, got up in a fabulous dress, dined out with Alexei, leaving him open-mouthed in admiration over her looks, her wit and her sex appeal.

'Let me see you,' Alexei urged, bending down to filch the sunglasses off her nose and inspect her battered face in the full unforgiving light of day.

Mercifully unaware of the heights her imagination could take her to, Alexei grimaced. 'Nasty. It'll be a few days before you look normal again.'

Billie snatched back her sunglasses and replaced

them on her nose with a shaking hand. His input on how she looked was overkill, for wasn't she already wincing over the rainbow bruising round her eye and the swelling distorting her face?

'Your mother's boyfriend is gone,' Alexei informed her.

Her brow furrowed. 'Gone? *Where?* What are you talking about?'

'I dealt with him.'

'And what's that supposed to mean?' Billie queried nervously.

'I took the launch back to the harbour with the doctor last night and confronted the man to tell him to leave.'

Billie rammed back her chair to stand up. 'You had no right to interfere!'

'Your mother is full of apologies but she caught the ferry with him this morning. The neighbours are up in arms and I think she decided that a short break from island life was in order.'

'Oh, my goodness!' With a groan of protest, Billie flung herself back down in her chair. 'What on earth did you say to Mum?'

'That if she ever hurt you again she would be charged with assault—'

A whimper of dammed-up fury and frustration escaped Billie. 'It was none of your business!' she bawled back at him. 'How dare you?'

'It's how we deal with problems on Speros—you know it is. Every community must have rules. Lauren's boyfriend could have raped you, although the neighbours are so nosy I think you would have been rescued before he got very far,' Alexei conceded with a gleam of dark sardonic humour in his unrepentant gaze. 'All that matters is that he is no longer on the island and he won't dare to come back.'

'But Lauren's gone as well, driven out of her own home!' Billie condemned emotively.

'Your mother will be back, don't worry. She's too clever to abandon the easy life she has here, thanks to you,' Alexei countered carelessly, his interest in the subject patently on the wane. 'However, I've come up with a solution to your problems.'

'I don't have any problems,' Billie told him stonily, abandoning the table and turning on her heel to head back at speed to her cabin.

'Billie!' Alexei breathed rawly. 'Get back here right now!'

Trembling with fury over his meddling in her private life, Billie was outraged by that glossy impenetrable Drakos assurance that made Alexei believe that he could do whatever he wanted to do, particularly on Speros. But the particular note of command in his strong voice stopped her dead. She could storm off but where to and why? They had gone toe to toe once before and, though she might have got her job back, she knew her tycoon boss well enough to know that it had been a one-chance-only deal. Slowly, as if every movement physically hurt, Billie turned round again.

'Finish your breakfast,' Alexei told her harshly, his exasperation unconcealed. 'We're leaving the ship in ten minutes.'

Clashing with the warning in his hard dark eyes,

Billie breathed in slow and deep, suddenly aware that the exchange was taking place right outside the office windows and marvelling that she could have forgotten the fact that they had an audience. Her spine as stiff as a steel pole, she took her seat again. A steward poured her tea and Alexei's coffee. She had to force herself to eat as all appetite had fled…

CHAPTER FOUR

A FOUR-WHEEL-DRIVE vehicle collected Alexei and Billie at the harbour. Billie was observing a rigorous silence.

'I've never known you to sulk before,' Alexei murmured with withering bite.

Her teeth were clenched together so hard that she was surprised they didn't chip. 'As far as I'm concerned you invaded my private life last night in a way that you had no right to do,' Billie responded brittlely.

Alexei closed a hard hand over hers and pulled on it to make her turn round and look at him. His heavily lashed golden eyes struck hers boldly head-on. 'I did what had to be done. You have no father, no brother, no other male relative or boyfriend, who can protect your interests. In their absence I count myself a friend as well as an employer. I took care of Dean Evans in a way that he understood.'

'And what's that supposed to mean?' A suspicion belatedly occurred to Billie and she gave him a shocked appraisal. 'Surely you didn't hit him?'

'Did you think that I would shake hands with him for

what he did?' Alexei flung his handsome dark head back, his stunning bone structure full of proud challenge. 'Yes, I hit him.'

In mute despair, Billie shook her vibrant head, the bright hair she had left loose to hide her swollen face behind rippling round her cheekbones. She said nothing, knew there was no point saying anything, and that any local man witnessing such an act the night before would have heartily applauded Alexei's violence. On every primitive masculine level, Alexei had been raised to react with the raw aggression of a caveman. Crossed in business, he hit back hard and his enmity was feared in the marketplace since he never forgot a slight. He would never turn the other cheek. He would find it impossible to forgive without having first meted out punishment.

'Well, I wish you hadn't got involved. I don't need anyone but myself to look after my interests.'

'You are very fortunate to have me,' Alexei responded as if she hadn't spoken and he gave her a glance of such fierce conviction and confidence in that statement that he left her bereft of speech.

When the four-wheel-drive turned off the road that followed the shoreline up a rough grassy lane, Billie frowned. 'Where are we going?'

The security guard driving them stopped the car and got out to open the door beside her, forcing her to climb out.

'I want to show you something…'

Billie swallowed a weary sigh, knowing better than to question a male whose every thought and idea seemed embedded in a driven need to make another fortune on top of the many he had already acquired. Walking into the sloping field, sheep scattering at their every step, Billie glanced in bemusement at Alexei. 'Isn't this too close to your family home for a tourist development?'

'I own this plot and I'm not planning a development here personally,' Alexei said drily. 'I'm offering it to you to enable you to build a house.'

Her green eyes opened very wide and she stared at him. 'I couldn't afford to buy this—'

'The plot would be a gift. From my point of view it would be convenient to have you living close by.'

'A gift? For goodness' sake, what would your family think?' Billie lifted an arm to indicate the fabulous view of the bay where the turquoise ocean below washed a long crescent of pale sand. 'A site like this must be worth a fortune!'

'I could give you a house in the village. Of course it would mean chucking out the existing tenants first.'

'Don't even think about it!' Billie shot back at him in horror.

'And a village house, even if there was one currently available, wouldn't address your problems.'

'For the last time, I don't *have* any problems!'

'You're too loyal to acknowledge the strife your mother creates for you, and as long as you live in the village you will still be dragged into Lauren's messy life. But if you have your own home at this end of the island, you will be left in peace,' Alexei pronounced.

There was a good deal of truth in what he had said and the idea of a private base where she would be far removed from Lauren's adventurous love life was a huge draw. 'I couldn't possibly accept a site from you. Your mother is already suspicious of me.'

Alexei laughed. 'So what? Live the life *you* want, not the life other people would lay out for you.'

'If only life were that simple…'

Alexei closed a strong hand over hers before she could walk away. Glittering golden eyes assailed hers in stubborn challenge. 'It is you who makes it complicated. I have more wealth than I could spend in a score of lifetimes. You need an independent home outside the village. You can build a house here and pay for it in stages. If you require finance I will give it to you. Your only other option will be to take up permanent residence in one of my family's guest suites.'

'But I'm hardly ever here!' she protested.

'That situation is about to change radically. My father is feeling his age and I have agreed to assume control of Drakos Shipping. I will be spending much more time on the island and you are my most trusted employee. So, cease this argument right now,' Alexei advised impatiently. 'You could make a proper home in this place. You know it makes sense.'

Her slender fingers flexed in the hold of his. His expectant gaze was on her, his domineering will bearing down on her like a powerful weight. She made a last ditch attempt to regain equality. 'If I accept the site, you will have to accept part ownership of any house that I build. That would be the only fair solution.'

Gazing down at her with deceptively indolent eyes of dark gold, a wicked slanting grin slowly slashed Alexei's wide sensual mouth. 'If I were to own a share of your house, it would give my mother sleepless nights!'

'But it would give me peace. I just couldn't accept the site as a gift. It's too valuable,' Billie told him in an urgent rush. 'You could explain the situation to her.'

'It is no business of hers.' Alexei stared down intently into the vivid little face so familiar to him that he could instantly discard any awareness of her bruises. Sincerity shone in her clear green eyes while her coppery hair snaked in bold strands across her cheekbones. No woman had ever fought to come up with a way of accepting a gift from him while returning the value of it. He wondered why money had less of a hold on her than on others of her sex. He wondered why he had never noticed before that she had a soft pink mouth as firm and luscious as a ripe peach. Hunger stirred arousal and a familiar delicious heaviness formed at his groin.

Billie felt the change in atmosphere with every fibre of her being but could no more have stepped away than she could have stopped breathing. His gilded gaze was mesmeric in its power to hold her. Her mouth ran dry, frantic tension holding her fast. The pool of liquid heat forming in her belly was sending an electrifying surge of responsiveness through her entire body, pinching her sensitive nipples taut, creating heat and dampness at the secret heart of her.

Alexei closed his arms round her. Cupping her hips with an intimacy that shocked her, he drew her up against his hard muscular length and kissed her. It was a kiss full of a passionate demand that rocked her where she stood. It was like being hit by lightning as she sizzled like meat under a grill and her knees almost crumpled beneath her weight.

It was Alexei's strong arms that kept her upright while he lightened the pressure of his intoxicating mouth and teased her reddened lips with tiny provocative caresses. Having reduced all resistance to rubble, he finally went in for the kill, dipping his tongue between her lips in a piercingly sweet invasion of her unbearably sensitive mouth and provoked a series of whimpering shivering gasps from somewhere inside her. It was the very first time she had experienced true sexual hunger and it was a raw need so powerful it rolled through her like thunder, blanking out all thought and control. For those split seconds she was both defenceless and aggressive, clinging to his lean hard physique, angling her head back to enable him, her entire body yearning for much more of the same.

'Will I be the first?' Alexei prompted in a roughened undertone.

'Yes,' she answered before she retrieved her wits and intelligence came back in a floodtide of anxiety and anger and regret. As she pulled free in response to those promptings the slivering pain of sudden separation from him cut through her as sharply as a knife.

Retaining a controlling grip on her slender hand, Alexei walked her back towards the car.

Billie hauled her fingers free of his. *'No!'* she protested strickenly. 'I don't want this!'

Alexei stilled and sent her a frowning look of incomprehension. 'What don't you want?'

'I don't want to be another notch on your bedpost.

Just roll back time a few minutes, *please*! The kiss didn't happen, forget it. You're my boss. I work for you… Neither of us wants to change that relationship!'

'You sound almost hysterical.' Hot golden eyes semi-screened by luxuriant black lashes, Alexei squared his aggressive jaw line. 'Everything changes, nothing stays static—that's life and you can't control it. You can't turn the clock back either. I want to take this attraction to its natural conclusion, *moraki mou*.'

'Only because you're not accustomed to any woman calling a halt…but I *am* calling a halt. I'm not like your other women…I don't do casual,' Billie proclaimed with proud vehemence.

'The spark we fired between us is too hot to douse,' Alexei delivered thickly, dark golden eyes locked to her like an incoming missile attack, making it clear that nothing she had said had impressed him.

'It was just sex,' she argued. 'And sex you can get anywhere with women far more beautiful than I am, so forget it and me in that line!'

'While I can still taste you in my mouth,' Alexei murmured huskily, shooting her a shockingly sensual appraisal that burned through her like a hot burning coal. 'I won't forget how you made me ache.'

'Stop it…' Billie raised her hands to silence him in a rare physical show of eloquence. '*Stop it!* It was a stupid kiss, a mistake, but it's not important and it's never going to happen again.'

Alexei stretched out his arms without warning and hauled her back to him, reconnecting her to the lean, tensile power of his muscular thighs and the potent thrust of his erection. Holding her entrapped, he stared down at her with all the cool of a predator stalking prey who knew he had all the time in the world. 'You can't tell me it's not going to happen again—that will only make me want you more.'

Awesomely conscious of the deep desperate longing still whirling inside her and crying out for satisfaction, Billie rested pleading green eyes on him. 'You know this is wrong. You know you would much rather have me working for you than having sex with you,' she told him feverishly.

'But having you fulfil both functions could well be an amazing tour de force,' Alexei countered with single-minded conviction. 'I would cut down on the other women.'

Billie almost screamed in frustration because no statement could have told her more clearly how out of alignment they both were. He was not only not getting her message, but also stubbornly refusing to listen to it.

'And that statement just shows how ill-suited we would be, because I wouldn't accept you having *any* other women! I wouldn't share you. No matter how many diamonds and treats you flung my way it wouldn't buy you back your freedom at the same time as you were with me.'

Alexei dealt her a lingering appraisal, searching her still-dilated pupils and the revealing redness of her lips while a rueful smile shadowed his beautiful sexy mouth. 'You're trying to scare me off—it's kind of sweet. But you know me better than that. When I want something I keep going until I get it. I don't switch off to order.'

'Was this all one big set-up, then? Is this why you're offering me this magnificent site to build on? Were you *trying* to buy me?' Billie flung at him in an emotional surge of accusation.

'You know me better than that, *moraki mou*. In any case, I'm more likely to give a reward to a lover at the *end* of the affair rather than at the beginning,' Alexei pointed out without an ounce of discomfiture.

Standing there in the sunshine, daring her censure, his lean bronzed features breathtakingly handsome, he could still take her breath away. Billie dropped her gaze and got into the car, wondering if the driver had seen that embrace, praying that he had not. If he had seen it, every member of Alexei's staff would know about it within twenty-four hours. The Drakos employee grapevine was terrifyingly efficient and the slightest hint that she was more intimate with Alexei than she ought to be would be sufficient to destroy the respect of her co-workers and her reputation.

'I've always been curious about you,' Alexei volunteered as the car took them back to the harbour. 'But I didn't suspect that we might be dynamite together.'

Curious? Would he make love to her out of curiosity alone? Sadly Billie thought that, yes, he would, for novelty attracted Alexei, who with every passing year became more bored with the myriad choices he enjoyed. Why the heck had she admitted that she was still a virgin? It was like whetting the appetite of a big game hunter with the offer of the ultimate quarry. After all, she was different and his lovers, strung across every continent, were almost interchangeable, she reflected tautly.

They were actresses, models or socialites, usually tall and blonde, always beautiful, sophisticated and aware that no woman held Alexei's interest for very long. They entered his life and left it again without causing a single ripple in his routine.

Only one woman had ever dented Alexei's ego and it had been Lauren who shared that story with Billie. According to island gossip, Alexei had fallen for Calisto Kolovos, the daughter of a rich manufacturer, when he was twenty-one years old. But all along Calisto had had another boyfriend: Xavier Bethune, a much older man who had been a good deal richer and more powerful than Alexei who, in those days, was still dependent on his father. Calisto was said to have married Xavier for his money and, ever since then, Alexei had had a heart of stone when it came to women. Billie was not naïve enough to believe that she could change him. She wanted more than sex from him and, if that was not forthcoming, valued her job more than any short-lived sexual fling that would only last long enough to satisfy his curiosity.

They boarded the yacht together. Tension was simmering like a hissing, boiling pot between them. 'Alexei…don't do this,' Billie urged half under her breath as they crossed the deck.

'Don't do what?' he drawled smooth as glass.

'It's not fair to put me in a position like this.'

His bold profile froze.

'I'm damned if I do and damned if I don't,' she continued awkwardly. 'I like my job. I want my life to stay the same.'

No woman had ever made a plea to his sense of honour on such terms and it infuriated him that Billie had done so; he felt she should somehow sense that the innate sense of integrity he possessed had the power to make him back off. Dark deep anger burning below the surface, for he was a man very much accustomed to getting his own way, Alexei murmured icily, 'I find it hard to believe that that is what you want.'

Billie looked towards the sun and wondered how much it resembled the male ego in size and brilliance. Alexei was a hugely powerful and wealthy man, made irresistible by his Greek-god looks and notorious reputation. Women had always wanted Alexei Drakos and it was a truth he had learned so young that her surrender could only seem inevitable to him. 'In the circumstances—my working for you,' she extended with care. 'I don't want anything to change.'

'So, if I sack you, I can have you,' Alexei pronounced flatly.

'You don't really want me, you know you don't. I'm not your type,' Billie reasoned in a feverish undertone.

'Make arrangements for a flight to Monaco for me and then take the next couple of days off,' Alexei instructed just outside the office, startling her. 'You were assaulted last night. You need recovery time. Naturally you can stay on board *Sea Queen*.'

And, that fast, she registered that he had listened to her at last. The strangest and most contrary sense of disappointment washed through Billie's taut figure. The excitement of the chase was over. He had loads of eager female connections in Monaco. Quickly, Alexei would move on, find a more willing woman and forget that he had ever thought she might be worthy of a fling. Her heart felt as if it were being hurled from a cliff down onto jagged rocks. She ignored that fact, her weakness; she had done what had to be done and it was time that she lived a more full life and found a man of her own to be with. In the course of her work, she had turned down many invitations because she had yet to meet anyone who could equal Alexei. But she would have to stop being so picky. By turning away from Alexei, she reminded herself firmly, she kept her excellent job and would hopefully also retain a good working relationship with him.

Alexei was less content. Since when had he, a Drakos male, allowed himself to be upstaged and outmanoeuvred by a female? But she had appealed to his conscience and, although it went against the grain to admit it, she had talked a good deal of sense. Wasn't that why he employed her? Common sense and calm distinguished Billie and until he had taken that kiss he would have sworn that nothing would faze her. But sex had splintered the calm and put her into retreat. She wasn't his type, he reminded himself impatiently while he showered later that day on board his private jet. She was just an employee and only in the very early days of creating his empire had he slept with women he employed. There were excellent reasons for respecting boundaries and, even as it was, Billie was always breaking through them and crossing the line. Was that why Billie was the only person in his life who had the power to make him feel human and real? She wasn't in awe of him, or his wealth or his status. When he had watched her eyes close in dreamy receipt of his mouth he had got a kick out of that susceptibility. At that moment, she had been with him every step of the way.

His brow furrowed. Why the hell was he even still thinking about her? His common sense and practicality did not seem to be the equal of hers, he registered grimly. His libido had him over a barrel. He would have sacrificed their working relationship in a second, had she been waiting in the cabin bed for him…and to hell with the immorality, inconvenience and poor long-term outlook of it all!

Three months after that day, Billie went out on a date with a charming Italian businessman called Pietro Castronovo. He took her out to dinner in a very fancy Florentine restaurant where she toyed with food that was too rich for her taste and tried to respond to his flirtatious chatter.

At ten o'clock, Alexei rang her and wrecked the evening. 'You should have checked with me before you went out. Pietro is a married man with two kids.'

'Thank you, sir,' Billie murmured flatly.

'I've got some work for you to do.'

'Right now, I'm on an evening out,' she responded thinly.

'Surely you're not planning on spending any more time with a married man?' Alexei enquired sardonically.

Billie came off her phone and apologised to Pietro for having answered it. 'I always take Alexei's calls.'

'You stand very high in his regard,' Pietro commented.

Billie breathed in deep. 'Are you married?'

Her companion's thin, good-looking face tightened and she knew the answer before he even parted his lips and acknowledged that he was. 'I should have asked,' she said ruefully. 'I wouldn't be here if I had known.'

Pietro tried to dissuade her from cutting the evening short, but Billie stood firm and wondered why she was so much angrier with Alexei than with Pietro. After all, Alexei's warning had been a timely one, coming as it did before she could get any more involved with the handsome Italian. But, somehow, being saved at the eleventh hour from a mistake by a male who had very few morals of his own simply incensed Billie.

When she returned to the penthouse hotel suite Alexei was occupying, Alexei was at work with the rest of the team. She sent him an accusing glance but would not have dreamt of telling him how she felt about his previous phone call in front of an audience. When the business was dealt with, he called her back before she could leave.

'Did you shake Castronovo off? He was born with the gift of the gab,' Alexei said very drily. 'I should have warned you about him.'

'I am able to look after myself,' Billie told him starchily. 'Thank you for the warning on this occasion, but please don't interfere like that again.'

'Naturally I interfered. I knew that you wouldn't intentionally date a married man.'

There was a little devil inside Billie's head and it deeply resented his assumption that she would never do anything untoward. 'Actually, that's not necessarily one hundred per cent true.'

'You were back at the hotel within thirty minutes of my phone call,' Alexei countered with dark amusement. 'Don't be ashamed of your principles. Too many people have none at all.'

And still she had wanted to slap him. Her long-overdue venture onto the dating scene had gone belly-up and left her with egg on her face. The person she most hated for his interference was, without a shadow of a doubt, Alexei. She would never choose to date another woman's husband, but Alexei had once again managed to make her feel a fool.

Eight months after that mortifying evening, Billie was in a better mood. She was sitting in her office in the Drakos villa on Speros, watching beautiful people through the windows. Got up in their fabulous evening outfits, the guests were laughing and drinking on the terrace outside the entertainment suite. The party she had arranged for Constantine's eightieth birthday was a huge success. Having made an appearance as instructed and stayed around long enough to check that the party schedule was running smoothly, Billie had bowed out to finish off some work.

In recent months her working hours had been very long, even though she now enjoyed the services of an assistant because her duties currently stretched to taking charge of Alexei's parents' social and travel arrangements as well. At the same time, she was making a hundred and one decisions about the building of her new house, which was currently two-thirds of the way towards being completed. She had picked the doors, the door handles, the bathroom and kitchen fittings and tiles. By spring the following year, she would be living under her own roof and could still hardly believe it.

In the planning stage the house had been a nightmare. Since anyone doing anything on Speros always looked first to the local community to supply services and skills, she had hired the island architect, Damon Marios, to design her new home. Damon, long since married and the father of two sturdy children, was still a friend. Alexei, however, had insisted on seeing the plans and changing things, pointing out that if he had an interest in the house, he also had the right to voice his viewpoint and ensure that the property was worthy of the site.

'I wanted something that fitted in with the island architectural style,' Billie had argued, fighting for the simple little cottage that Damon had designed.

'There is no style here. A century ago, dirt-poor people built dwellings that were the cheapest of the cheap,' Alexei had derided, urging Damon to use a little creativity and open up windows and doors to the fabulous views in a much more contemporary—and expensive—approach.

'Plain can be stylish,' Billie had said sharply.

'No wonder people talk about you and Alexei,' Damon had remarked in the aftermath of hearing that rough-edged exchange of views between them. 'I can't believe the way you argue with him.'

'It may be an unconventional working relationship but it works well for us,' Billie declared lightly.

It had been easy to silence Damon, make him cloak the curiosity she saw in his eyes, for he was too polite to persist. She was accustomed to being questioned about Alexei and her relationship with him. Just about everyone was madly curious about Alexei: how he lived, what made him tick, his women, his houses, his yachts and his sporting prowess. He provided an endless stream of fascination for others. Since he had taken the helm of Drakos Shipping, he had become a hugely powerful tycoon. The richer he became, the more the media wanted to know about him and the less they found out, because Alexei didn't grant interviews. Paparazzi lay in wait for his every public appearance but his brutally efficient security team barred and evaded their invasions. Some of his lovers had, of course, gone to the press to sell stories, acts of betrayal that had only increased the level of interest in him and his lifestyle.

'Billie!' A voice intervened, separating Billie from her thoughts and making her look up from her computer screen to smile in some dismay at the slender brunette in her fifties framed in the doorway. 'I knew you would sneak off to work!' Natasha Drakos scolded. 'Come back to the party, *please*.'

Billie surrendered gracefully; Alexei's mother was a strong-willed woman. From the moment Alexei had taken over the family shipping business, Billie had started working long hours in the office suite at the Drakos villa and inevitably the two women had got to know each other better. While her son flew one woman after another out to Speros for entertainment during his hours of leisure, Natasha had soon realised that she had nothing to fear from Billie and had been considerably more concerned about some of the wilder females in her son's incomparable little black book.

Billie, a slim, vibrant figure in an apple-green dress, reflected that she had had to build an armour-plated shell to cope with the heartache of constantly seeing Alexei with other women. Her sole consolation was that none of them seemed to have the power to hold onto him for very long. But constantly controlling her thoughts, reactions and expressions in Alexei's radius was a strain. Even now when she was chatting to his mother about the party, Billie was already bracing herself for a glimpse of Alexei with his current love, the English socialite Tia Flint.

Alexei was so tall that it was the work of a moment to pick him and Tia out of the crowd. Tia, an eye-catching blonde in a black glistening sheath dress, was wound round him like a vine. Billie studied Alexei, noting the stubborn angle of his strong jaw and the distance in his brilliant dark eyes. Tia was giggling and gesticulating with her hands to a bunch of friends nearby. In his tailored dinner jacket, Alexei looked as coolly beautiful and remote as a classic bronze statue.

'Tia is on the way out,' Natasha forecast knowledgeably. 'He's bored.'

'Maybe,' Billie responded, watching the way Tia's fingers were smoothing across Alexei's shirtfront with the familiarity of a lover. It hurt her to look, yet some awful fascination prevented her from snatching her gaze away.

As the hostess drifted off to relocate her husband Damon crossed the floor to greet Billie. 'You owe me a dance.'

Billie tensed because Damon's wife, Ilona, was the possessive type. She had visited the site on several occa-

sions and had made it clear that she wanted to be sure that
any interaction between her husband and his former
school friend remained strictly related to business. 'Do I?'

'Sorry, Damon, you missed the boat a long time ago,'
Alexei breathed sardonically, stepping between them
without warning and closing an arm round Billie to
sweep her straight out onto the dance floor.

'What on earth are you doing?' Billie gasped, thoroughly taken aback by his sudden appearance and that
crack that harked back nine years to her first crush as a
schoolgirl.

'Saving your good name,' he censured with a curled
lip. 'Damon's wife took the kids and went home to her
parents last week. His marriage is over. Damon making
a beeline for you is a bad idea as you'll get the blame
for breaking them up.'

'You couldn't care less about my good name,'
Billie riposted.

Hooded dark golden eyes dropped to her tense
heart-shaped face. 'Damon's looking for consolation,
so give him a wide berth. Remember the guy who cut
you dead on the ferry all those years ago. You look
sexy in green—'

'Out of line, Alexei,' Billie framed, wildly aware of
the strength and power of his tall, well-built body
against hers and the hand splayed to her taut spine. She
was barely able to breathe for nerves. 'Where's Tia?'

'With her friends. She's drunk and angry I won't go
to the races with her next week. Organise a flight home
for her tomorrow.'

'Yes.' So, Tia was yesterday's news. However, the effervescent blonde had lasted six weeks, which was a good month longer than many did.

The hand at her spine eased down to her derrière. Heat curled in her pelvis, her breasts stirring within the confines of her bra, the nipples distending in response.

'Oh…look at your parents out on the terrace!' Billie suddenly exclaimed, and she stilled to watch the older couple dancing outside alone. 'They're really enjoying their party.'

Alexei lowered his arrogant dark head, his breath fanning her cheek. The familiar scent of him, a specific aroma composed of warm husky male and the designer cologne he wore, assailed her nostrils and sent an arrow-sharp dart of longing through her. If he came too close she suffered that instinctive response half a dozen times in her working day. The awesome physical awareness he could inflict on her was terrifying.

Alexei held her back from him the better to look at her. Simmering dark golden eyes roamed over her like caramel melting on a hot day, burning everywhere his gaze touched. 'Stop trying to change the subject,' he husked. 'The way that fabric clings to your breasts is indecent and very flattering.'

And she glanced down and saw that her prominent nipples were clearly visible beneath her frock. Mortification engulfed her like a tidal wave. A hot pink flared up below her fine skin and washed her face with colour. Turning on her heel, she walked off the floor, furious with him, furious with herself. He was baiting her. He knew she was still attracted to him and he used it like a weapon against her. But she shouldn't have reacted.

The party, Billie decided ruefully, would be fine without her. She smiled at the touching recollection of Alexei's parents wrapped in each others' arms as they danced alone outside. It did not occur to her, nor indeed to anyone else that evening, that this image might be one of the last she or they would ever have of the older couple…

CHAPTER FIVE

THREE weeks later, the news of the tragic accident came in a devastating phone call. Helios, the head of Alexei's security team, phoned Billie. It was the middle of the night and she was half stupid with sleep when she answered. He repeated the details slowly and with great sorrow. After a stunned pause, she asked him why he had not rung Alexei direct.

'You know him well. You are a woman—you will break the news better,' Helios opined heavily. 'It is a terrible thing.'

'I'll go and speak to him.' Finger-combing her hair off her brow with a shaking hand, Billie got out of bed and pulled on the wrap lying on the chair. She did not dare wait to wash and brush up because time was of the essence. She literally ran down the passageway to his bedroom and knocked loudly on the door before opening it.

The light went on by the bed, Alexei lurching up against the pillows, black hair spiky and tousled, a heavy shadow of stubble obscuring his jaw line, while a tangle of black chest hair rioted across his superb masculine torso. She suspected that he wasn't wearing a stitch of clothing.

'What's up?' he asked thickly.

'Helios phoned. Your parents…'

'My parents…*what*?' Alexei rasped at her as if some sixth sense had already kicked in to forewarn him that she had bad news to break.

'They were involved in a motorway pile-up. They're in hospital in Athens. It's very serious,' she told him carefully.

She watched his bright eyes darken and the sudden spread of pallor below his bronzed skin now pulling taut with tension across his high cheekbones. He thrust back the bedding in a violent movement. 'Are they alive?'

Hastily she spun away and turned her back to him before he could cross the room naked in front of her. '*Just*. There are no details yet. I'll contact your pilot—'

'Make the arrangements,' Alexei bit out.

'Do you want me to come with you?' she prompted.

'Of course, I bloody well want you to come!' Alexei launched back at her rawly.

Tears of shock and compassion ready to overflow from her eyes, Billie sped back to her room, tore off her night gear and yanked out a business suit to wear. It was only forty-eight hours since they had arrived at the chateau Alexei owned in the South of France. While Alexei toured the vines and the state-of-the-art winery he had created and enjoyed long technical discussions with the vintner he had hired, she had relaxed from formality and worn cropped linen trousers and a casual T-shirt to wander around the lavender-edged borders in the idyllic garden that thrummed with visiting bees and humming birds. Just hours earlier that combination of sunshine and scented flowers had struck her as the purest taste of heaven but now those feelings were being utterly swept away...

Alexei was unusually quiet during the flight, his dark mood weighting the atmosphere. There was a mention of the accident on the news but no names were released. Somehow word of the high-profile victims had escaped, however, for the hospital was already under siege by the press when they arrived. For the first time ever, though, a path through the crush of paparazzi that led all the way to the entrance cleared in front of Alexei. In the foyer they were greeted by the chief administrator and a doctor who answered Alexei's questions about Constantine and Natasha's conditions. Alexei's mother had sustained a serious head injury and was on life support. Constantine had already had emergency surgery and remained very weak. The prognosis was not good for either of them.

Reluctant to intrude, Billie hung back as it slowly sank in that Alexei's mother was in a coma from which she was unlikely to recover. She was shocked by the sight of the vivacious older woman lying so still in her hospital bed. After sitting by Natasha and talking to her for a while in an effort to revive her, Alexei hurried on to his father's bedside. Constantine roused and gripped his son's hand and words were exchanged but within the hour the old man suffered a massive heart attack and passed away. Mid-morning, Alexei was present when his mother's life support was switched off. Billie's heart bled for him but he remained fully in control. They left the hospital by a back entrance and drove out to a private airfield to board a helicopter. His mobile phone was ringing incessantly by then. He answered the first few calls from relatives, explained what had happened and then he gave the phone to Billie to look after. By the time they landed back on Speros, he was grey with grief and exhaustion.

The household staff, some of whom were openly crying, awaited Alexei's arrival in the hall of the villa. Alexei talked to all of them. By then, Billie was fielding calls from chief executives and lawyers, wanting to know what was going to happen in a hundred different areas. She told them all that they had to wait. Alexei needed peace in which to grieve and while he wandered round the huge rambling villa like a lost soul Billie made the funeral arrangements.

The following few days were very stressful. Great-aunts, great-uncles, aunts, uncles and cousins travelled from all over the world to the island, packing out the villa just when Alexei would have preferred time alone. Television channels were running documentaries based on old grainy newsreel coverage of Constantine's life and various marriages. The media was responding with a similar slew of articles. Although the funeral was to be strictly private and for family and close friends only, several of Alexei's former lovers arrived uninvited. It was Billie's job to send them packing again and after being treated to a fit of hysterics by Brigitte, a French singer, that left her ears ringing, she was desperate to escape the hothouse feel of the villa and went off to visit her mother for a couple of hours.

After the Dean episode the previous year, Lauren had spent quite a few weeks in London staying with her sister, Hilary. Once off the island, Lauren's relationship with the toy boy had disintegrated fast. She had phoned her daughter several times to say sorry and although Billie fully believed that she had forgiven Lauren she now saw less of her mother and avoided her altogether when she had a man in tow.

'I had a walk up to see how that fancy new house of yours was coming on,' Lauren told her. 'It's going to be quite something—no wonder the locals are talking!'

Billie tried and failed to resist her curiosity. 'What about?'

'What do you think? We all see the fancy women in Alexei's life in the newspapers and the magazines, but you're the only one to get a building site within walking distance of the Drakos villa. Everyone knows you work very closely with Alexei and enjoy a lot of privileges— naturally some people think that you're earning the extras on your back!' Lauren supplied with a crudity that made her daughter grit her teeth together.

'It's not like that between us.'

'But not for want of you wishing,' Lauren needled, casting a shrewd eye at Billie's pink cheeks. 'I'm not so stupid that I haven't noticed how you feel about him.'

It was not a conversation Billie wanted to have with Lauren, who had never been very good at keeping secrets. Her mobile phone rang and she answered it as a welcome distraction, wandering to the other side of the room and switching to English when she recognised the upper-class English vowel sounds of Alexei's great-

aunt, Lady Marina Chalfont, his father's half-sister.
Lady Marina was stranded in Athens. Billie was happy
to sort out transport for her, not only because the older
woman was in her eighties but because she was Alexei's
favourite relative.

'You're on duty twenty-four-seven,' Lauren complained.

'It's not quite as bad as that,' Billie declared, pressing
a kiss to her mother's cheek before leaving an hour later.

But nonetheless that was how it felt when Billie
returned to the villa and discovered that chaos had de-
veloped in her absence. Alexei strode into the entrance
hall, lean darkly handsome face hard with anger and
frustration. 'Where the hell have you been?' he demanded rawly. 'I'm trying to work and the phone is
ringing off the hook. Your assistant is an idiot and my
cousins are doing a conga through the house!'

'I went to see my mother.'

Like a storm cloud, Alexei shrugged his dismissal of
that as an acceptable excuse and strode back to the
office suite in high dudgeon. A moment later, the conga
crew passed Billie by and she intervened. Alexei's
cousins, many of them just teenagers, were keen to treat
the funerals as an excuse to enjoy some sun, sea and
sand and were striking a very wrong note in the grieving
household. It took all of Billie's tact to soothe everyone
down before a major row broke out. Chastened, the
young people went down to the beach in pursuit of more
acceptable entertainment.

Her assistant, Kasia, was swallowing back tears
when Billie joined her and she confessed that in certain

moods Alexei scared her. Everyone on the business team kept their head down when Billie arrived and she knew that Alexei had been letting everyone feel the rough edge of his often sarcastic tongue. Alexei's great-aunt arrived soon after in the helicopter Billie had despatched to pick her up.

'Go and see Marina settled,' Alexei commanded her. 'It's you she will want to see.'

'I'm not in the mood right now.'

Billie breathed in deep to restrain herself but still couldn't hold back the words bubbling into her mouth. 'Maybe it's time you got in the mood. Lots of people badly want to speak to you. Tomorrow will only be more difficult if you don't make time for some of them now.'

An unearthly silence spread like a cloaking cloud of poison gas through the large office. There was a palpable air of shock. Alexei lifted incredulous dark eyes of hauteur to Billie's unrepentant face. Ducking his searing gaze, she spun on her heel to leave the office.

An instant later he was walking by her side. 'Don't you ever speak to me like that again,' he warned her icily.

'You know perfectly well what you should be doing.'

'You have no idea what I'm going through,' Alexei condemned.

'Oh, yes, I have,' Billie fielded ruefully, for nobody who had witnessed the camaraderie between Alexei and his parents could have failed to notice how very close the trio were. Like many only children, Alexei had spent a great deal of time with adults and his childhood as such had been short-lived. His father had been taking him on guided tours of super tankers and oil refineries by the age of five. Independent though Alexei was, his parents' deaths had left him like a ship without a rudder.

Billie showed Lady Marina, the tall and imposing daughter of a countess, into the most spacious guest suite. 'How is my nephew?' the old lady asked fondly.

'He's coping very well—'

'Which for a Drakos male means he's not coping at all,' Marina interposed with a shake of her elegant white head. 'Constantine always froze too when an emotional response was demanded. Is Alexei using work as an escape?'

Billie folded her lips and nodded.

'Alexei's in shock. Drakos men aren't used to problems that they can't solve, situations they can't fix. He needs to go wild for a while, get it all out of his system. Holding it all in is unhealthy.'

Billie almost smiled at that unlikely idea because, while the tabloids might once have depicted the fabulously wealthy Drakos heir as a wild, undisciplined playboy, Billie had learned that even though Alexei might break the rules and flout the conventions he always acted with forethought and he never, ever relinquished control. He also rejoiced in nerves of steel and the sensitivity of a granite block.

But what she saw later that evening when Alexei had abandoned his social mask shook that conviction. Unable to find him to pass on news of an unexpected movement on the New York Stock Exchange, she finally ran him to ground in the special conservatory that housed his mother's prized collection of tropical orchids. She hovered outside, watching him through the glass as he stood there and trailed a long lean finger down the stem of a white waxen bloom. He had never had any interest in the flowers that had fascinated his Russian mother, and neither had his late father. Indeed both men had regularly teased Natasha about her obsession. But, for all that, a year ago Alexei had financed an Amazonian plant collectors' trip, which had resulted in his mother having a newly discovered orchid named after her. Natasha had been thrilled beyond belief at having such an honour conferred on her.

Billie's gaze flicked up to Alexei's bold brown profile and froze at the sight of the glisten of moisture highlighting his hard cheekbones. Silent tears were rolling down his face. She could *taste* his sadness, his regret for times past never to be regained. Her throat thickened, her own eyes wet, and she looked hurriedly away, feeling that she could not possibly intrude on so intensely private a moment in which he believed himself alone and unobserved. But, oh, how she longed for the right to push open that door and hurry to his side to offer him comfort! But freedom of expression was not part of her role and she reluctantly walked away while scolding herself for having underestimated the depth of Alexei's loss and his feelings. His tough self-discipline had fooled even her, persuading her that he was totally in control and that business would pretty much go on as usual. Why else had she chased him down to talk about his US Stocks? She left a note on his desk but it was a long time before she got to sleep that night because she was far too busy wondering when Alexei had last slept.

The following day was an extremely busy one for Billie. The security precautions to ensure the interments remained private were rigorous. Constantine and Natasha were laid to rest in the walled cemetery behind the village church. Alexei, who always rose highest to a challenge, shook off the moodiness and silences of the day before to act as gracious host at the villa. Special travelling arrangements had been put in place to enable the guests to leave in good time for their flights home.

Once everyone was gone, an unearthly silence spread through the house because most of the staff was now off duty as well. Billie went off in search of Alexei because after working so many hours at a stretch she was keen to have some time that was her own. After all, tomorrow would bring an early start, the reading of the will and a return to business, which promised to be even more challenging than anything that had gone before. But who could tell what mood Alexei would be in? Only since the motorway pile-up had she truly appreciated just how volatile he could be

Alexei was on the terrace with a drink in his hand. He had gone through most of the day that way and the sight of that ever-present glass struck a wrong note for her because overindulging in alcohol was not the norm for him. She recalled her painful glimpse of him with his mother's orchids the night before and compressed her mouth. He had discarded his tie and unbuttoned his shirt but he still wore his black designer suit with striking panache. As she looked at him, taking in the grim gold of his stunning eyes and the rough shadow of stubble darkening his jaw line, her heart skipped a beat and she felt horribly guilty for reacting to his sexual allure on such an unhappy day.

'You need a drink,' Alexei drawled.

'No, thanks…er—'

Alexei strode past her into the house. 'What would you like?'

'I don't drink when I'm working—'

'If I'm not working, you're not working either,' Alexei traded and slowly the stiffness in her bearing eased.

'Rosé wine…'

'Rosé? You've got no class,' Alexei groaned from indoors.

'I only like sweet drinks,' she confided.

'Relax, take off your jacket,' Alexei told her.

And she did because she was too warm. Her sleek grey silk T-shirt complemented her tailored skirt. She had learned how to put together an outfit for work and was satisfied that she looked elegant, while being less confident of what she wore outside working hours. A moisture-beaded glass clasped in her hand, she studied Alexei, long dark lashes veiling her anxious green eyes from the disturbing penetration of his.

'You put on a hell of a show for my family today. I appreciate it.'

Her cheeks warmed. 'Thanks.'

'I just wish I felt a little happier about having left my mother in her final resting place down by the church.'

Billie frowned. 'Sorry, I don't understand.'

'I'd always planned to take her away travelling once my father was gone,' Alexei confided with a raw, roughened edge of emotion to his voice. 'I waited too long. It never occurred to me that they might die at the same time. When she married my father she gave up her youth. She spent thirty-odd years withering with boredom and frustration on this island. Speros was her cage, her punishment for marrying a man in his fifties who was afraid that she would meet someone else if he let her have more freedom. She deserved better.'

'Your mother always seemed happy.'

'She was a great wife and mother.' Alexei downed the contents of his glass in a salute. 'But she got very little pleasure out of being a Drakos.'

'You and your father—her family—meant everything to her,' Billie responded softly, and then she set down her empty glass. 'I'm going to turn in now.'

'You have to be the only woman in my life who continually tries to walk out on me,' Alexei remarked with a wondering shake of his handsome dark head. 'Any idea why that is?'

And all over again Billie felt the intense charismatic pull of him tugging at her senses. He was gorgeous and she would have had to be bereft of her senses not to appreciate him. His high-voltage sensuality was like a honey trap, she reasoned feverishly, and not one she could afford to fall into again.

'Working for you is tiring,' she fielded awkwardly.

'What a drab description of being in my employment,' Alexei countered, his Greek accent and possibly the amount of alcohol he had consumed making the words slur together.

Meeting his brilliant golden gaze, Billie felt like a rabbit caught in car headlights: paralysed, trapped and befuddled by the blinding brightness.

'It's never boring and I enjoy the travel and all the

different people I meet,' she conceded in a small tense voice. 'Perhaps you should have allowed Brigitte to stay on today to keep you company.'

'The French one who screamed abuse at you when you told her she couldn't stay? You've got to be kidding!' A familiar pulse of arousal was making Alexei uncomfortable. There was something about Billie that turned him on and he had long since given up trying to work out what it was. Yes, she had beautiful green eyes, clear fine skin and a peach of a mouth, but she wasn't in his class and he knew it. She had nothing in common with his other lovers either—that would be a ridiculous comparison to make. Yet, somehow, he was always aware of the movements of that small, delightfully curvy body when it was in his vicinity. He never failed to notice the luscious curve of her breasts and the firm feminine swell of her bottom below a fitted skirt. And, just at that moment, with his blood running insanely hot and making him hard as steel, he wanted to strip off her clothes and sink hard and long into the silky welcome of her virginal body.

'You shouldn't be alone tonight.'

Alexei reached out and closed his lean brown hands over hers to tug her closer. 'Ah-h-h, that's sweet, Billie. Do you really think I need emotional support from anyone?'

'Well, you're unlikely to find it at the foot of a bottle,' Billie told him with unhesitating disapproval.

Lounging back on the edge of a stone table with his long, lean, powerful thighs spread wide, Alexei flung back his handsome dark head and laughed with rich appreciation of that reprimand. His hands tightened over hers swiftly when she made a move to break free. 'Only from your lips, *moraki mou*. The unblemished truth.'

'Don't call me "my little baby",' Billie urged with complete seriousness. 'It's that sort of talk which gives people the wrong idea about our relationship.'

'But you *are* very small,' Alexei riposted with dark amusement, his rich drawl running the syllables of the words together as he thought it was funny that she never seemed to notice the effect she had on him. 'I'm not accustomed to little women.'

'That's not the point.' Lifting her head, Billie encountered scorching golden eyes framed by luxuriant black lashes and registered that looking at him directly was seriously unwise. She felt the heat of that appraisal right to the very core of her, setting up a string of little sensual shocks that tightened her nipples and made her uncomfortably conscious of the uniquely sensitive area between her thighs.

'The point here…' Alexei breathed silkily as he flexed his strong hands and inexorably drew her closer still '…is that I want you and you want me and we've been dancing round that fact for far too long.'

Billie was as unyielding as a cliff face being buffeted by a high wind. 'That's not true.'

'Stop being stuffy,' Alexei urged, his intonation soft and sibilant, black-lashed stormy golden eyes threatening to reel her in like a fish on a line.

'I'm not being stuffy. I'm just stating a fact,' Billie told him tartly. 'Last year I got a bit of a crush on my boss but I got over it—I'm sure you've had loads of female staff who over time became attracted to you.'

'But none who tasted as hot as you,' Alexei slotted in dangerously. 'So you got over me?'

Billie nodded vigorously, glad he had made that very basic but crucial connection. *'Totally.'*

Alexei leant forward and slowly, sensually captured her lips, suckling their ripe curves before sliding his tongue moistly into her mouth in an explicit thrust. And she couldn't breathe for excitement and felt her legs wobble like crumbling supports. He caught her to him with strong arms, hands splaying across her bottom. Trembling she came up for air and gasped, 'We *can't*—'

'Ne, ne, we can,' Alexei asserted thickly. 'No more games.'

Resistance had hitherto been ingrained in Billie, but, although she dug deep, this time she couldn't find a trace of her usual caution. Games? The very word offended her. Was that what he thought? That saying no had merely been an exercise cynically staged to increase his desire for her? She refused to believe that he could see her in that light because her own feelings were so different. In his arms she ironically felt ridiculously safe. There had been no other man in her life for three years. She loved him and he would never need her more than he needed her now. Like a battery-operated doll able to go in only one direction, she let her swollen mouth brush back across his, her entire body tingling with sexual longing. Being touched by him, even having the right to hold him close, lent a whole new exciting dimension to her feelings for him that went to her head like strong drink.

He carried her past the swimming pool terrace to the

guest suite she was occupying until her house was ready for her. Automatic lights flashed on at every step to illuminate their progress.

'What about tomorrow?' Billie asked with sudden urgency.

'Who knows?' Alexei breathed in a tone of dismissal. 'Right now I don't want to think about today or, for that matter, tomorrow, *moraki mou*.'

Her slim fingers brushed his cheekbone in a soothing gesture of tenderness. 'Then don't think about them,' she whispered softly…

CHAPTER SIX

'IF YOU only knew how long I have dreamt of doing this with you…' Alexei groaned, settling Billie down on the bed and pausing only to shed his jacket and shoes before joining her there.

Billie was mesmerised by his intrinsic poise, for he seemed as at home in her bedroom as in his own. Indeed, lounging back against her pillows, Alexei was a beautiful fantasy that didn't seem quite real to her. His black hair and sun-darkened olive skin were an eye-catching contrast against the pale bedding. It was a challenge for her to drag her gaze from the exotically high cheekbones, dramatic deep-set dark eyes and arrogant nose that gave such strength and character to his lean, handsome face. The sensual side of her nature had finally run away with her, she acknowledged in a rush of dismay. Did that mean that she was more like her highly sexed mother than she had ever appreciated? That fear tormented her but one kiss had mown down her defences and turned her into a pushover.

'You don't believe me,' Alexei accused.

'Does it matter?' Billie wouldn't look at him. Thoughts of her mother's chequered love life had cast a sleazy shadow over her. Perhaps Lauren had also thought that she loved the first man in her life. Would Alexei simply think she was cheap and easy if she slept with him? With a past like his, she could hardly expect to stand out from the crowd.

'With you? *Yes*,' he told her bluntly in English for emphasis.

'I don't need empty words and promises.' Billie made a valiant attempt to suppress her insecurity and turned towards him, green eyes darkened to emerald by her yearning and the terrible guilty sense that she was breaking every one of her rules. Yet when she met those heavily lashed golden eyes, it struck her that rules were made to be broken and that, for her, Alexei Drakos would always be an exception. He laced long brown fingers slowly into the tumbling fall of her red hair, smoothing and fanning the vibrant strands across his palm in the lamplight in a move that accentuated the different shades.

'I never found red hair attractive until I saw yours glowing in the sunlight with all those crazy streaks of copper and gold and bronze,' he admitted, before he jerked her head back and took a hungry driving kiss that exploded through her wound-up body like a depth charge.

The renewed taste of him was a wake-up call to her slumbering senses. That kiss was insanely stimulating. Indeed the probe of his tongue sent a spasm of fierce sexual need spearing right to the heart of her, releasing a feverish energy that pulsed through her receptive flesh in a sensual wave. Alexei pulled back from her to remove her T-shirt, an action that left her blinking in surprise like an owl suddenly thrust into bright light.

'You're always wearing too many clothes, *moraki mou*. I can't wait to get them off,' he confided thickly, one lean hand already engaged in unzipping her skirt so that he could slide it off her as easily as if she were standing up.

Uneasily conscious of her body's semi-clad state in a serviceable black cotton bra and panties, Billie went stiff and self-conscious. She was hopelessly convinced that he was sure to notice his mistake now when he discovered that—shock! horror!—her garments did not miraculously conceal a designer-thin body with dainty breasts and legs as long as a giraffe's. She knew that though there was nothing wrong with her figure it was very ordinary, and while she might be undersized in the height department she certainly wasn't in her bust or hip measurements. Her face was scarlet with self-consciousness.

'I have a huge sense of anticipation,' Alexei revealed, reaching for her bra, his attention welded hungrily to the snowy hillocks firmly encased in black cotton.

'But anticipation often leads to disappointment,' Billie warned him worriedly, pushing his arms back so that she could start unbuttoning his shirt and occupy her trembling hands. She was desperate to conceal her nerves and her sheer embarrassing ignorance of such intimacies. 'It's my turn.'

'Always the pessimist and so democratic,' Alexei mocked.

Billie was very well aware that she was dealing with

an autocrat, who had learned in the cradle that he had no need to share anything with anyone. Her fingers were clumsy on the buttons of his shirt and to complete her task she daringly yanked the garment free of his belt. Deep down inside her head, a frightened voice was wailing, 'What on earth are you doing?' over and over again. Black hair curled over Alexei's powerful pectoral muscles and arrowed down over his taut abdomen to vanish from view below his waist. He was a hot but sexually intimidating vision and he took her breath away.

With an unhurried hand he unhooked her bra and trailed it off. Billie had to fight a powerful urge to try and cover her breasts with her hands like some shocked maiden from an old comedy film; her skin had never felt so naked or exposed.

'You're magnificent,' he told her in Greek 'Lush…'

And the taste of that word resonating in the silence made her tremble, while his almost reverent finger brushed the prominent bud of a pouting pink nipple adorning her voluptuous blue-veined flesh. He bent his dark head and closed his mouth to that tantalising peak, rolling the unbearably tender bud between his lips while he used skilled fingers to administer similar pressure to its neglected twin. Pushing her back on the pillows, he cupped and squeezed her plump breasts, stroking them while he suckled ever more strongly. Swiftly he plunged her straight into a storm of new and almost painful sensation. Her nipples throbbed from his attentions and tugged internal strings that seemed to be connected to even more intimate places. Her hips lifted, her thighs pushing together to contain the tension between them. Little animal sounds escaped low in her throat. All of a sudden she was in a place she had never been before and feeling things she had never dreamt she might feel. That it should be Alexei taking her to that place blew her away.

'You're so different from the women I'm used to, *moraki mou*. And differences are always exciting,' Alexei husked, tugging up her knees and skimming off her panties in one easy movement before dispensing with his trousers and casting them aside.

That statement had unsettled Billie as much as the all-male bulge of arousal defined by his silk boxers. 'How am I different?' she pressed in a small voice.

In the midst of an assessing visual sweep of her body, Alexei suddenly smiled down at her with the wicked charisma that was so much his own. He made no attempt to hide the hungry appreciation in his dark golden eyes. 'Everything about you is one hundred per cent real…the colour of your hair, your breasts. Nothing is fake and nothing has been remodelled.'

Beneath that powerful appraisal, Billie could still only blush and she was so painfully uncertain and shy that that betraying tide of colour even engulfed the pale upper slopes of her breasts. 'Here I am, flaws and all,' she said valiantly. 'I can only assume I take after my father for, let's face it, I inherited none of my mother's genes!'

'Your attributes are much more subtle,' Alexei interrupted, discarding his boxers.

'But I really would have loved the blonde hair and long legs,' Billie confided shakily, using humour to try and hide her vulnerability while trying not to stare fixedly at his manhood, which was of more threatening masculine dimensions than she had expected.

'Blonde hair and long legs are easily found. I prefer you just as you are,' Alexei husked, running a forefinger down between her breasts and over her quivering stomach to the triangle of dark red hair at the junction of her legs.

Billie stopped breathing while her heart hammered at a frantic rate. He found the sensitive swollen bud below the curls and gently massaged it, releasing a rolling tide of sweet sensation that stole the breath from her lungs. She could feel her insides dissolving to honey even while a burn of greater need flamed into being. Her slender thighs parting, she shifted against his knowing hand, her hips developing a motion all of their own because she could not contain the intensity of what he was making her feel. As he explored the delicate pink folds of flesh she had exposed and pleasured the hidden opening to her womanhood she writhed, out of control and breathless.

'You're so tight and wet,' Alexei growled with raw satisfaction. 'Are you still a virgin?'

Eyes wide and green and feverish against the hectically flushed oval of her face, she nodded confirmation. 'Does it matter?'

'Oh, yes. It matters to me, *moraki mou*,' Alexei told her in Greek. 'A more honourable man would walk away, because I'm not making you any promises.'

'I know that.' Billie was quick to dispel any suggestion that she had such expectations, yet the denial was like a stab at her heart.

Simmering golden eyes fringed by inky black lashes assailed her. 'But, for what it's worth, I feel more of a connection with you than I have ever felt with a woman. Somehow we fit, *khriso mou*. I respect you. I like you. Everything feels natural with you, nothing forced or false.'

'It's just all the emotion of the last few days,' Billie protested, fearful of allowing herself to believe that anything was happening between them that could mean something to him, because she thought that such a conviction could only lead her to the madness of false hope and disillusionment. 'And the alcohol.'

'The...*alcohol*?' Alexei carolled in disbelief. 'Are you suggesting that I might not know what I'm doing?'

'I don't want to take advantage of you,' Billie said deadpan.

Laughing uproariously, Alexei pulled her to him and held her close to kiss her with a hungry passion that was passionately free of restraint. The sexual heat flowed through her again while he strung a line of provocative kisses down the extended length of her throat and across the alabaster slopes of her breasts. She was boneless, breathless even before he returned to the hot dampness between her legs. With exquisite skill, he toyed with the satin flesh, probing the delicate entrance where she ached for a fulfilment she had never known before. His sensual onslaught was a sweet torment, lighting up her every nerve-ending with longing. Her excitement built and built to a towering height and she couldn't stay still or silence the tiny gasps and whimpers breaking from her lips.

He put a pillow below her hips and came over her

with practised ease. 'I'll try not to hurt you,' he promised thickly. 'But I want you so much I'm in agony.'

Feeling him nudging at the entrance to her body, she tensed. He urged her to stay still and as relaxed as possible before he sank his engorged shaft slowly into her tight inner channel. She was lost in the extraordinary feeling of his erotic invasion. A flicker of discomfort came as a warning before the main event, when he plunged deeper into resisting flesh, and she yelped at the flash of pain, only to be mortified when he stopped.

'No, don't stop…just get it over with,' she mumbled through gritted teeth.

'How can I resist such an invitation?' Alexei groaned, pausing to brush his lips across her brow in a comforting motion before driving deeper until her body yielded and sheathed him completely. Becoming accustomed to that sensation of fullness, she shifted her hips and as swiftly savoured the flood of intense erotic feelings roused by his slow, steady movements. She brought up her knees, lifting her hips to accommodate his thrusts and crying out her pleasure in encouragement. He abandoned his control, sliding his hands below her to lift her even higher and deepen his penetration, his heart labouring against hers. He ravished her with long driven thrusts and sent her excitement climbing so high she screamed when she tipped over the edge into an explosion of ecstasy and wild ripples of sensual delight gripped her quivering body in the aftermath.

'Bliss…for the first time I see the point of your name, *khriso mou*,' Alexei breathed from the rumpled depths of her hair, slowly lifting his tousled head to gaze down at her with wondering appreciation. 'That was amazing, but—'

'But?'

'We have just had sex without precautions. I can assure you that I'm clean. I have regular check-ups and I have never until this moment made love without a condom.'

Billie was much more tense than Alexei, whose big powerful frame was comparatively relaxed against hers. *'Without?'*

'We should have gone back to my room. What part of your cycle are you in?'

Embarrassed by the enquiry and rigid with apprehension, Billie had to think and then they had to count, a pastime that Billie was much better at than Alexei, whose unusually slow mental arithmetic only reminded her that he was very far from being sober. Although she was in the second half of her cycle, he decided that there wasn't much to worry about. Billie was, however, less sanguine, momentarily picturing the horror of conceiving a child by a male who revelled in his freedom and who wouldn't want an illegitimate kid or its mother.

Claiming a hot, driving kiss, Alexei coaxed her out of that pensive mood. He shifted against her, cupping her hips to bring her into contact again with his renewed arousal. Billie was startled, not having realised that he might be ready again so quickly or even that he might want to repeat the experience. 'It was so good I can't wait to do it again,' Alexei told her raggedly, his hands straying to more sensitive places to lessen any reluctance she might be suffering from.

Billie was astonished by how fast he could make her

want him again even when she was a little sore. She melted below his urgent kisses. He put her in a different position on her side and made love to her slowly and provocatively, driving her to an even more earth-shattering climax the second time.

'This is crazy,' he acknowledged lazily in the aftermath. 'I'll have to go and get some condoms. I don't want to get you pregnant.'

'We're being very irresponsible,' Billie agreed breathlessly, so limp, weak and mindless after that last wave of pleasure that she could barely speak.

'That's what I like about you, *khriso mou*,' Alexei husked, brushing aside the dark red damp hair at the nape of her neck to kiss the tender skin there. 'You bring out another side of me, an irresponsible side. I'm different with you.'

The mattress gave as he slid out of bed and she flipped over with anxious eyes. 'Where are you going?'

'The shower, then to my room to take care of the contraception.'

For a couple of minutes, Billie lay on the bed as though she were welded to it. Shock was sinking in fast and filling her with apprehension and doubts. Although she had sworn that she would never be foolish enough to sleep with Alexei, she had just done so. In fact she had taken part in a shameless sexual romp that was indefensible for, while she might love him, he did not love her. What price now her long-held secret belief that she was somehow morally superior in her restraint to her mother? That she was different? More sensible, more steady? Shame drenched her in a tide of drowning regret. As far as Alexei was concerned now, she would just figure as one more in a long line of willing bed partners...

'Billie?' Alexei called, startling her.

'What?'

'Come and join me,' Alexei urged impatiently.

In the shower? In no immediate hurry to extend her sexual education, Billie slid uneasily off the bed and padded into the en suite, snatching up a towel from the doorway and holding it against herself.

'Drop the towel,' Alexei exclaimed, making her jump as he rammed back the glass door to survey her with a raised brow of enquiry.

Her heart was beating frantically fast as her fingers released the towel and he smiled, a slow burning smile that turned her heart inside out. Later she had no recollection of moving forward to join him in that glass cubicle. He soaked her hair and ran the soap over her voluptuous figure with lascivious thoroughness. As he teased her she became less self-conscious and was still giggling when she watched him pull on trousers over his boxers.

Alexei extended a lazy hand. 'Want to come with me? We could spend the rest of the night in my room.'

Thinking of all the women he had entertained there and the household staff who would soon register her presence in their employer's bedroom, Billie shook her head, her amusement killed stone dead in its tracks. It would be like announcing their intimacy and the news would go round the island faster than the speed of light. Lauren would smirk at her as if she had known all along that her daughter was a fool. 'I'll wait here for you.'

'Lazybones,' Alexei mocked, tugging on his shirt and thrusting his feet into his shoes.

Bare-chested, his hair spiky from the shower and with a heavy growth of black stubble on his handsome face, Alexei resembled a very sexy pirate. Her heart pounded as hard as if she were running a marathon. The instant he stepped out of the bedroom into the adjoining reception room that formed part of the guest suite she was gripped by a strong sense of loss. Soon it would be dawn, soon the night would be over—would what they had just shared die along with the night hours? Filled with dismay by that enervating suspicion, Billie scrambled out of bed, pulled on her wrap and went after him.

As she left the bedroom she heard Alexei vent a startled curse in Greek and then there was a noise she didn't recognise, followed by silence. She hurried to the door that opened out onto the pool area and stared in horror at the sight of Alexei lying flat on the concrete, apparently having fallen down several steps. Her handbag lay on its side just outside the door. Oh, dear heaven, he had tripped over it!

'Alexei! *Alexei?*' she cried, kneeling down beside him and registering that he was unconscious.

Rising swiftly, she went to phone for help when a groan emanated from Alexei. Quick as a flash, she rushed back to his side. He was sitting up, clutching his head.

'Alexei? Are you all right?'

'Billie?' He focused on her with clear difficulty, a dazed aspect to his eyes. 'What happened?'

'You tripped and fell.'

Alexei levered himself upright, brushing down his

clothes, and even though he was swaying he began walking back in a wavering line towards the main house.

'You should lie down for a minute.' She hurried ahead of him to open the door he was heading for and rested her hand on his arm before he could pass her. 'Let me call the doctor.'

'The doctor? What are you talking about?' Alexei countered flatly, frowning down at her restraining hand. 'I don't need a doctor.'

'You knocked yourself unconscious for a couple of minutes and it's always advisable to consult a doctor in those circumstances,' Billie pointed out anxiously, withdrawing her hand after the look he had given her. Only minutes ago he might have been sharing a bed with her, but her gesture had clearly struck him as too familiar by far. 'A head-scan might be a good idea as well.'

'Stop fussing, Billie. I'm not in the mood.' Alexei raked the black hair back off his face in a gesture of exasperation. 'My hair's damp and I'm not wearing any socks. I must have gone for a swim. That'll teach me to drink—I don't remember and I might have drowned myself.'

Billie frowned and looked down at her bare feet. He thought he had gone swimming? He didn't remember. 'What's the last thing you recall?'

'Talking to Marina after the funeral,' he breathed tautly. 'I don't want to think about all that right now.'

'I know, but the fact that you can't remember everything means there's something wrong. You're confused,' Billie stated tightly.

'Don't be ridiculous,' Alexei derided. 'I'm not a child and I'm not confused either. I had a few drinks too many and now I'm paying the price for it. No offence intended, Billie, but right now I'd prefer my own company.'

A painful flush washed her heart-shaped face as if he had slapped her. That colour slowly waned to leave her pale as she looked steadily back at him. There was nothing there in his lean, hard-boned visage: no tenderness, intimacy, or even awareness that anything might be lacking. He had forgotten her as easily as one forgot a bad dream or something trivial. And, on a Drakos male's terms, a fleeting sexual episode *was* of the utmost triviality.

'Goodnight,' she said shakily. 'But I still think you ought to see a doctor.'

Already halfway across the salon, Alexei was no longer listening. For several minutes, Billie simply stood there, barefoot and naked but for a thin wrap. For the space of that time she couldn't believe that he had forgotten her and walked away with no intention of coming back. She imagined following him into his bedroom, telling him that he had made love to her, but what use would that be if he could not even recall the incident? Wouldn't she look pathetic? As if she was chasing after him?

But wasn't it downright dangerous that he was refusing to seek medical attention? He had hit his head hard enough to lose consciousness, however briefly. Obviously he had sustained an injury. It had been early evening when she saw him talking to his great-aunt, Lady Marina. He was suffering from a loss of memory but evidently convinced that, rather than amnesia caused by a head injury, an alcoholic blackout was at fault.

Was it all right to leave him alone to go to bed? Anxiety fingered down her taut spine.

Billie knocked on Alexei's bedroom door. She was about to repeat the action when it flew open.

'What?' Alexei demanded curtly.

'Are you sure you're okay? No headache? Nausea? Dizziness?' she prompted.

'Go back to bed and stop fussing round me like a mother hen!' he urged with unhidden impatience.

Tears stinging her eyes at that label, which was about as far removed from sexy or desirable as could be, Billie did as she was told. Tomorrow morning though she would ring the village doctor and tell him about Alexei's fall.

Her bedding carried his scent and she buried her nose in a pillow and cried. Was it ridiculous to wonder if his forgetfulness regarding that crucial few hours could be subconsciously deliberate? Maybe he had forgotten about going to bed with her because he didn't want to remember that it had happened. And maybe fate was giving her a second chance, for what he didn't recall she didn't have to worry about. Now she could just go on as if nothing had happened, with the added comfort of not having to fret about what he thought of her for sleeping with him in the first place. Her job was safe.

But no matter how hard Billie worked at putting a positive spin on his inability to recall their short-lived intimacy, she failed to find solace in the fact. And the fear that he might have suffered a more serious injury than he was willing to consider destroyed her ability to sleep. So great was Billie's concern on that score that she phoned the village doctor as soon as the surgery opened and Dr Melas agreed to come up to the villa and check Alexei out…

CHAPTER SEVEN

BILLIE was so tense that even the shallowest breaths were rattling through her lungs at too fast a rate. Lean, strong face set in grim lines, Alexei was seething with her and every inch a Greek tycoon in his proud bearing.

'You overstepped the mark. You skirt it all the time but today you went too far,' Alexei delivered in a tone of rebuke and command that was still raw-edged with anger. 'This is your last warning. Nobody is indispensable, so, if I once gave you the impression that you were, wipe that assumption from your mind. For what I pay you, I could find someone else equally efficient—'

'Yes, yes, I'm sure you could,' Billie inserted, her skin clammy with nervous perspiration, for he had never before spoken to her in such a tone or studied her with such censure.

'Don't interrupt me when I'm speaking!' Alexei launched down at her crushingly.

Billie buttoned her mouth up tight and gritted her teeth. She could feel the tears building up behind her eyes, tears of chagrin and hurt and shock at being treated like a lowly office junior who had messed up spectacularly.

'I did not need or wish to consult Dr Melas this morning. And even had I needed to, it was for me to make that decision,' Alexei imparted succinctly. 'You wasted the good doctor's time. You lack perspective with regard to your role as an employee.'

Billie swallowed back angry defensive words and said with a determined lack of emotion, 'I was genuinely concerned about your health.'

Alexei dealt her a cold appraisal that cut her to the bone. 'That's way beyond your remit.'

'Yes. It won't happen again,' Billie told him woodenly.

Her colour high, she walked straight-backed back through the general office past the business team, who must have heard Alexei raise his voice to her, and returned to her office. Her only consolation was that Dr Melas had called in to talk to her before he left to stress that, although he had got nowhere with Alexei either, she *had* done the right thing in phoning him. He too wanted Alexei to see a neurologist and have a scan. Of course, wasn't Alexei just being his usual nonconformist self? Too stubborn to play safe and too convinced of his superhuman health and higher intelligence to take advice from lesser mortals? So that was the end of that road. She had overstepped her boundaries. For the moment, Alexei had forgotten their hours in the guest-suite bed. Would he ever remember? And did she even want him to?

His father's sudden death had left a couple of important business deals wide open and Alexei went straight to New York with his team to handle the fallout the next day. He stayed there for over a week, putting in workaholic hours, and followed it up with a similar week in London. Being left alone on the island shook Billie, as Alexei rarely left her behind. Her assistant, Kasia, had crumpled under the pressure of working for Alexei and had used her position as a springboard into a less taxing job elsewhere. Billie had yet to hire a replacement. Convinced that a break from her usual routine would do her good, she set off on a quarterly visit to a number of Alexei's European properties, where she checked out problems, new staff and authorised essential maintenance. She was in Venice, at his ancient palazzo, when Alexei decided to take some time off and cruise the Caribbean in his yacht, *Sea Queen*. He invited friends on board and several long-distance photos of gorgeous bikini-clad women appeared in the newspapers. Billie's heart sank like a stone and when she found herself poring over those pictures with a magnifying glass to see if she recognised any of the faces, she realised that jealousy and fear were eating her alive.

Yet how could she fear losing what she had never had? There was no commitment and no security in being a one-night stand. She'd had her moment and it had lasted for even less time than she might have hoped. And even while she scolded herself for being so foolish, she recognised that she already had a much more serious issue to worry about: her menstrual cycle had stopped dead in its tracks and her period was overdue.

That reality struck horror into Billie's bones. Furthermore, there was no way she could go down to the village pharmacy and purchase a pregnancy test or visit the doctor without the fear that her movements might become public knowledge. While she trusted Dr Melas, she had less faith in the other surgery staff with access to medical records. Juicy gossip on the island had a way of bypassing all the rules of confidentiality and travelling faster than the speed of light. For that reason, Billie caught the ferry to Athens and bought her pregnancy test there, carrying it out in the privacy of the small hotel room she booked for the night. The result was positive.

In complete shock she sat on the side of the bed and studied the test wand, her green eyes darkening with panic and pain. *Now what?* Nothing would ever be the same again, she acknowledged sickly. The child of a single parent, who had often mourned the lack of a father in her life, Billie was utterly devastated by this positive confirmation. From her teen years, she had prided herself on her common sense and the restraint she had utilised to ensure that she did not make the same mistakes as her mother had. But, even so, in spite of her awareness of the pitfalls of an unplanned pregnancy, here she was, just like Lauren, alone and pregnant by a man who had made no commitment to her. Her life was suddenly going badly wrong and it was all her own fault for sleeping with Alexei. Billie was appalled by her predicament.

And practising a conveniently short memory in respect of Alexei's amnesia would no longer be possible: *he* had made her pregnant. Sitting on the edge of the bed, she rocked back and forth in an unconsciously self-soothing motion while shame, self-loathing and regret flooded her. She had thought she was so clever, but she hadn't been half clever enough when it came to looking out for herself and her own interests. They had both been very foolish that night in letting passion triumph to the extent of running the totally unnecessary risk of her conceiving. Now, unhappily, it was evidently time to pay the piper and her reputation, her entire career, were dead in the water. Everyone would think that Alexei had always used her as a convenient body in his bed between affairs and just as many would think she had contrived to fall pregnant with an eye to the main chance. Mortified by that prospect, she breathed in deep. He was due back on Speros the next week and she would have to tell him. What choice did she have?

That it might not be that clear-cut a question became clear during the subsequent days. Panos phoned her from the yacht to ask her to transfer some computer files that were required.

'Not that I really think we're likely to need them with the boss otherwise occupied,' her colleague groaned.

'What's he occupied with?' Billie prompted as her fingers flew nimbly over the keyboard while she searched out the requested files.

'Not what, *who*,' Panos corrected wryly. 'There's a new, demanding lady on board *Sea Queen* and all of a sudden business is taking a back seat. We won't be back tomorrow. The cruise is being extended.'

In response to that announcement, Billie's heart started thumping very, very fast, her skin turning clammy. Of course she had guessed that Alexei would soon find a new woman but the reality of it actually happening hurt like hell. In fact she felt as if someone had knocked her chair over and sent her to the floor with a bone-jolting crash. 'Who is she?'

'An old flame, but one from well before my time—tall and blonde, with the looks of a supermodel... Calisto Bethune, recently divorced,' her colleague supplied.

Already winded by that metaphorical crash, now Billie felt as if she were being brutally kicked. She recognised that name, recalled the gossip. Calisto was possibly the only woman alive who had ever passed over Alexei in favour of another man and now it seemed she had returned to take a second bite from the same apple. Gripped by an awful obsessive need to know more, Billie got busy on the Internet and checked out Calisto. Now the childless ex-wife of a Swiss electronics tycoon, she was truly gorgeous, with a perfect face and a perfect body and a similar heritage to Alexei's own as she was from the upper echelons of Greek society.

Back on Speros that night, Billie phoned her aunt, Hilary, in the UK and talked until she was hoarse about what she had done and how it had all gone hideously wrong. As the sad tale unfolded Hilary made sympathetic sounds and exclamations that allowed Billie to feel that she was no longer quite as alone as she felt.

'I've been worrying about something like this happening for a long time,' her aunt confessed ruefully. 'You're in love with Alexei Drakos and were probably putting out encouraging signals. An opportunistic male like him was certain to take advantage at some stage and the night of the funeral was a given...'

'I just wanted to *be* there for him…'

'Well, don't be too tough on yourself. Plenty of women have dreamt that same dream as you.' Hilary sighed with something less than tact. 'But what's done is done. Now you need to decide what you want to do and you have to spell out what happened that night to Alexei. Embarrassment shouldn't come into it. You and that baby you're carrying need support.'

But in the days that followed, nausea began to surface when a certain smell or taste made Billie's newly sensitive tummy roll and sent her rushing to the cloakroom. She came no closer to the answer of what to do next: to try to make such a revelation to Alexei on the phone struck her as out of the question, but the prospect of flying out to the yacht to break such news with his latest lady in residence seemed even more inappropriate. Increasingly, references to Calisto Bethune began to appear in the gossip columns and were soon accompanied by photos of what was referred to as the 'loved-up couple'. Billie saw a photo of Alexei and Calisto walking hand in hand, both of them tall, beautiful and coolly fashionable, and she thought sickly that the pair looked so well together that they might have been a match made in heaven.

Barely twenty-four hours after Billie had pored with agonised eyes over that picture, wondering if she had ever seen Alexei look so relaxed, he returned to the villa, having flown himself home in a helicopter. He strode into the office, black hair tousled by the breeze, his lean, dark, devastating face intent. There she was at her desk, her bright head inclined to her computer

bearing that knowledge from the sidelines of his life, but the concept of him loving one of his female entourage was more than she could stand.

'Congratulations.' Billie was pale as milk and she spoke with a fixed smile while she fought with all her might to conceal and dampen her true feelings of bitter jealousy and resentment. 'I assume you're talking about Calisto Bethune. I'm very happy for you both. Have you set a date?'

Alexei released a husky laugh and spread his hands in an immediate silencing motion. 'I'm not moving quite *that* fast, Billie. We're back together and that happened quickly enough. That is more than sufficient for the moment.'

Billie breathed again at that evidence of native caution while he went about giving her instructions for the party he wanted organised to officially introduce Calisto to his family. With her dark auburn head bent, she took rapid notes from Alexei while he stood by her desk. The aroma of the peachy scent he always associated with her assailed his nostrils. He thought it was soap or shampoo, rather than perfume, and he had always liked it. He found himself gazing down at the pale crescent of skin exposed at the nape of her neck. That little bit of bare skin exuded an oddly erotic appeal. For a split second he was tempted to bend down and press his mouth to that delicate fine-grained flesh that never took any colour from the sun. The urge made him tense in surprise and frown.

Straightening, he strode over to the French windows overlooking the flower bedecked terrace and superb gardens beyond the glass. There was a heaviness at his groin, a ready sexual urgency that startled him. Was it simply a reaction against the relationship he had recently revived? Too much familiarity and proximity could breed more than contempt, he acknowledged wryly. What had come over him? It was a source of pride to him that, with the exception of one weak and curious moment when he'd kissed her, he had never hit on Billie. He was fond of her, had always been fond of her, and he looked out for her much as though she were one of his youthful cousins. There was an innocence about Billie that he had always cherished.

Long after he had gone, Billie sat there wondering what theme the caterers would dream up for the Drakos family bash. It was to take place in London. She would ask if she could take that weekend off to see Hilary. Alexei would definitely not want her baby now and that conviction cut through her like a knife, sending a shard of pure panic travelling through her. The timing of her conception could not have been worse; it might wreck his romance if Calisto realised that she would not be the mother of his firstborn child.

Did that mean that she should keep quiet? Could she rise above her jealousy enough to let Alexei and Calisto continue to enjoy their happiness in finding each other again? She knew she wasn't prepared to have an abortion. That option had been discarded early on, even though she had not yet admitted it to Hilary, who had become the safe repository for most of Billie's turbulent thoughts and feelings. But surely her only other choice was to give up her child for adoption? That was another painful sacrifice she could not face. After all, she might not be able to have Alexei, *but she could have his child*.

And if he had no memory of sharing her bed, he would have no suspicion that he had fathered her baby. On the other hand, she reflected ruefully, he would be so shocked by her having a child out of wedlock that he would not rest until she had told him who the father was. He might have accused her of overstepping the line but, in truth, it had always been Alexei who was most inclined to interfere in *her* private life. Furthermore, if she wanted to keep her baby, how was she to afford to do so?

She earned a terrific salary, but she had poured every cent she earned into the building of her house, the price of that project far exceeding the original estimates. For the next year her earnings were committed to completing the house, which would be ready for occupation in six months' time. A house she could never sell except at a bargain price, for all island property had to be offered to the locals first and it would be too expensive for most of them to consider. With single parenthood staring her in the face she could not afford to write off or sell her only asset at a huge loss, particularly when Alexei's generous gift of that plot of land with panoramic sea views had to be reflected in ensuring he received a fair percentage share of any sale.

In short, Billie appreciated she was financially trapped on the island of Speros for the foreseeable future. She could not jack in her job either while she needed to settle the bills for the house. Her *dream* house, she reflected painfully, had suddenly become a burden, an anchor tying her to a place and a job that she now wanted to leave. After all, how could she stand by and watch while Alexei romanced and married his long-lost first love? Getting ready for bed that evening, she studied her still-flat stomach with anxiety and wondered how much time she had before her condition became obvious.

Hilary was not impressed by her niece's arguments against making Alexei aware of her pregnancy. 'So, he's spoken for now, well, bully for him!' she snorted the following night when Billie phoned for a chat. 'But he still has a big responsibility towards you and any other woman he impregnates!'

'Legally, yes, but I don't want or need his support…'

'Don't be so proud that you cut off your nose to spite your face,' Hilary pleaded. 'It's unfortunate that at this point he's met another woman and it seems to be serious, but that is not your responsibility.'

'He's happy. I don't want to wreck it,' Billie confided heavily. 'In addition, since he's forgotten what happened that night, telling him and convincing him will be a very undignified battle…'

'Even a Drakos can't fight a DNA test,' Hilary opined. 'Perhaps it would be as well to wait until the baby is born before making a claim.'

'I really don't want his money, Hilary. I'm more concerned about finding a way to keep my baby and stay in my job.'

'But how on earth could you do that and work at the same time? If you're thinking of Lauren helping out, I don't think—'

'Of course I'm not—'

'If only it was me that lived on the island and not my

sister, the problem would be solved,' Hilary commented.
'I would love to look after your baby.'

'Well, you could if you were willing to move out
here. My new house has plenty of room. Of course you
couldn't leave John,' Billie realised, referring to her
uncle who was living in a care home where Hilary
visited him almost every day.

'John might not be here for much longer,' her aunt
divulged tautly. 'He's fading away before my eyes.'

'I'm so sorry,' Billie responded, having also refused
to think about the near impossibility of concealing her
baby's parentage if she tried to raise her child on the
island. 'I was lost in this wonderful daydream of having
you here on the spot, instead of thousands of miles
away. I was being silly.'

'No, if it wasn't for John, I would agree like a shot.
I would just love a fresh start, new faces, new pos-
sibilities…' Hilary confided breathlessly.

The germ of an audacious idea came to Billie. 'I
think I know how we could do it and nobody would ever
be able to guess that it was Alexei's baby.'

And that was the moment that the plan of concealment was born, laid out at first to an unimpressed Hilary,
who thought her niece was utterly crazy to suggest such
a thing; there was no question of Hilary leaving her
sick husband alone in the UK. 'But who would ever
believe that your baby was mine?'

'Why not? You're only thirty-eight. Nobody here but
Lauren knows about John's illness,' Billie argued with
growing enthusiasm. 'And we wouldn't have to live the
lie for ever, Hilary. Once I'd saved enough money up,

I'd sell the house and find another job and we would leave the island with the secret intact. But there would be no need to continue the pretence once we settled somewhere new—'

'Even if I was ever in a position to help you, Lauren would know we were lying—'

'I'm sure we could persuade Mum to keep quiet. Hilary, if it was possible—it would allow me to keep my baby without causing a big furore,' Billie reasoned fiercely. 'Please think it over and say yes.'

'If it's what you really want, I would do it simply because I love babies and I'd love to live on the island. But not while John is still alive. He may not recognise me most of the time when I visit,' Hilary admitted painfully as she referred to her husband's dementia, 'but he does have occasional moments when he's quite lucid. I know he hasn't long left but let's not talk about the impossible right now.'

'No, let's not,' Billie said, guiltily aware of her insensitivity.

'I don't understand how you're planning to hide the fact that you're pregnant from Alexei,' Hilary declared.

'I'll conceal it for as long as I can and then I'll ask Alexei to give me a career break so that I can return to England to stay with you for a while. It's a reasonable request.'

'If you give birth here you could leave the baby with me to look after. I haven't been able to find another permanent teaching job yet and I could manage fine,' her aunt asserted. 'It wouldn't be easy for you to leave your child behind with me but I'd love him or her like my own.'

'I know you would,' Billie replied warmly.

Billie slept right through that night for the first time since she had discovered that she was pregnant. In the dawn light she wakened and ran back over the plan, worrying over the weak spots while wincing over the idea of plunging both herself and her aunt into living a lie. No solution would be perfect or foolproof, she reasoned frantically, but one that ensured her child enjoyed loving care and security would definitely be worth bending a few rules for. She splayed her hand over the deceptive flatness of her stomach. She wanted to keep her baby; she wanted her unborn child very, very much. In the short term, if nobody was harmed by her concealing her secret, surely a few lies could be no great sin?

The next day, Damon Marios asked her to meet him at the site of her new house to discuss the terrace. She had hired him to not only design her new home, but also as project manager to supervise the building, ensuring that she endured minimal disruption to her life. In the slumberous heat of the afternoon, Billie drove up the rough gravelled lane and parked at the edge of the site beside Damon's SUV, wondering how she would ever turn the baked-dry dustbowl of her surroundings into a garden.

'I thought we'd have some lunch while we talked,' Damon remarked, a smile on his handsome face as he indicated the picnic lunch already artfully arranged in the shade of a gnarled olive tree.

'Oh…what a lovely idea,' Billie said in surprise, lowering herself down onto the rug with a soft sigh. Damon offered her food while trying to persuade her to do something more elaborate with the terrace than had been planned. 'The views are so spectacular,' he pointed out.

Billie breathed in deep and shook her head at the wine he offered in favour of the bottled water. 'I'm afraid I want the house finished as soon as possible and I would prefer not to incur any extra expense. I do still have to furnish it!'

Scanning the taut pallor of her face, Damon frowned. 'You've been so stressed these past weeks, Billie. What's wrong?'

His perceptive powers were unwelcome and her face tightened and she munched busily at her sandwich, finally pausing to murmur, 'Nothing's wrong. The summer heat here sometimes tires me out—that's all.'

'Alexei does like to get his pound of flesh. I don't know how you stand the pace. And if the press are on the right track, he's got that bitch Calisto back to keep him busy.'

Billie stiffened. 'Why do you call her that?'

'If she is back in Alexei's life to stay, you'll soon find out. According to my mother, Calisto was horrible to the household staff at the villa last time around…a real diva. There's also a rumour that his parents disliked her so much they threatened to disinherit him and that that's why she married Bethune instead.'

'People change and she was young,' Billie said wryly.

Damon reached for her hand. 'We used to be close friends, Billie.'

'I hope we still are.' Billie gently slid her hand free again.

'But I'd like us to be something more than friends,' Damon was honest enough to admit as he retrieved her fingers with dogged determination.

And it was at that opportune moment that Alexei strolled out of the back of the house and stood lazily studying them from the shadows. Black hair swept back from his brow, sunglasses anchored on his arrogant nose and sheathed in a soft grey summer-weight suit, he was as stylish and sophisticated in appearance as a model on a cat walk. 'Don't mind me,' he urged silkily. 'I thought it was time I came for a look around.'

Instantly, Damon released Billie's hand and sprang up. 'Let me give you the official tour.'

'I didn't hear a car,' Billie commented.

'I walked over from the villa,' Alexei fielded, eyes framed by dark-as-midnight lashes skimming over her blushing face. 'Sorry if I interrupted something.'

'You didn't,' Billie countered flatly, tugging her skirt down to her knees and reaching defiantly for another sandwich.

The two men walked round the house while Billie sat outside in the shade, fed up with both of them as she listened to snatches of their revealing dialogue. Damon was so deferential around Alexei that he set her teeth on edge and Alexei had no business declaring that a larger terrace was a necessity, rather than an extravagant extra. And what was Damon playing at? Why did men always refuse to take no for an answer? How many times did she have to tell him that she wasn't interested now in dating him?

Alexei reappeared and asked her for the keys of the car she had driven over, which did after all belong to him. 'Come back with me. I have some calls for you to make.'

Ignoring Damon's look of disappointment, Billie

scrambled up and smoothed down her skirt. Red-hot temper made her hands tremble a little. It was not that she wanted to stay and risk encouraging Damon, it was resentment at being smoothly manipulated into doing what Alexei wanted her to do.

'You're about to overstep the boundaries again,' she warned Alexei fiercely as she climbed into the hot car with him.

'He's not the guy for you. A bloody picnic on a building site…' he breathed with incredulous derision. 'How cool is that?'

'If I listened to you, I'd never get a guy! Every time one comes near me, you interfere and stick a spoke in the wheels. I'd like to know how you justify that when I'm not even allowed to call a doctor if you hurt yourself!' Billie launched back at him in an angry hail of words that she shot at him like bullets.

'You can trust me to put your interests first,' he drawled with unblemished assurance, his bold bronzed profile relaxed. 'Damon will most probably end up returning to his wife and children. Don't get caught up in their drama.'

'Working for you I've got enough drama of my own!' Billie bawled back at him, turning up the air conditioning with an impatient hand, ignoring it when he winced at the furious rush of icy air directed at him. 'You have no right to interfere. I'm an adult entitled to make my own mistakes. Stay out of my private life!'

And she sat there thinking how ridiculous it was for her to argue with him when she was carrying his child, to be able to shout but not to tell him the truth. But he would pity her if he knew the truth and he would feel very guilty. She knew him well enough to make that forecast and although her heart ached inside her like an open wound she was painfully aware that neither his pity nor his guilt, and certainly not his money, would provide her with the smallest comfort...

CHAPTER EIGHT

IN THE weeks that followed, Billie began to gather unwelcome information about Calisto Bethune, a woman she had never met who, it seemed, had a way of making her mark wherever she went. Calisto trod on toes without fear, she hurt and insulted with constant criticism, she demanded and screamed abuse if she didn't get what she wanted fast enough. Sooner or later, all staff complaints about Calisto ended up on Billie's desk. It seemed to her that every employee who came into too close contact with the gorgeous blonde whom Alexei was planning to marry hated her.

'If you're not prepared to make an official complaint, there's nothing I can do,' Billie told a sobbing stewardess from the yacht. 'Mrs Bethune is Alexei's partner. You'll have to get used to her ways.'

'She's so rude. I'm not her slave! If she speaks to me like that one more time, I'm quitting!'

'You could make this complaint official,' Billie pointed out for the third time.

The stewardess grimaced. 'I don't want anything on

paper…you know Mr Drakos has promised my brother
a job when he finishes school. I wouldn't want to take
the risk of offending him.'

Billie suppressed a sigh, for she had heard it all
before too many times. Nobody ever wanted to annoy
Alexei. Everyone wanted to stay on the right side of
him. It meant that he sailed through life on a sea as
smooth and flat as glass, protected from the ripples and
storms that lesser mortals endured.

The chef on *Sea Queen* had already quit after a volley
of censure from Calisto over a meal she had disliked. One
of Alexei's most choice and favoured employees, the
chef had long had secret offers from others keen to poach
his renowned skills. When Alexei professed surprise that
Billie had not contrived to dissuade his chef from leaving
his employ, Billie decided to be more honest.

'Your girlfriend offended him. I tried to persuade
him to stay but he wouldn't change his mind.'

'Calisto is very forthright.'

'The chef isn't the only one of your employees with
a problem with that,' Billie dared.

Every inch an arrogant Drakos in his bearing, Alexei
lifted a questioning ebony brow. 'Are you saying that
there have been complaints?'

'Nothing official, but some employees are finding her
manner hard to handle.'

Alexei compressed his wide sensual mouth into a forbidding line. 'Then they'll have to learn to be less sensitive. I won't tolerate disrespect towards her.'

'Of course not,' Billie declared, inwardly castigating
herself for not having the gumption to warn him that

Calisto was a demon with staff and that few would long withstand her vicious temper and verbal abuse. No doubt when people began to leave he would get the message, but there was no way that Billie could bring herself to be more frank right now.

'How are you feeling?' he asked.

'Me?' Billie questioned in surprise. 'Why are you asking me that?'

Alexei released his breath in an impatient hiss. 'Anatalya told me that you've been unwell for quite a few weeks. I would have preferred to hear that from you.'

Billie's face flamed and then lost colour again. Her entire skin surface dampened with nervous tension below her clothing. How foolish of her to overlook the likelihood that the housekeeper would notice the attacks of nausea she had tried so hard to conceal!

'Did you consult the doctor?'

'Er…no,' she admitted grittily.

'So I'm not the only person around here who avoids medical advice,' Alexei noted mockingly.

'I caught a bug and it took a while to shake off. That's all,' Billie retorted with a jerky lift of her shoulders that dismissed the topic as trivial. 'I'm fine now.'

That weekend she flew to London to check that the events planner, Janine, had all the arrangements in hand for Calisto and Alexei's party. The ballroom of Alexei's town house was exquisitely decorated for an event that promised to be the most fashionable of the season. Billie checked her profile in a mirror, noting with relief that the loose jacket of her suit still concealed her thickening waistline and softly curving stomach. Mercifully,

she had got over her nausea and at three months
pregnant was now anxiously noticing that the changes
in her shape were beginning to accelerate. She reckoned
that within another six weeks other people might begin
to suspect her secret. Within the next fortnight she would
have to tackle Alexei about her proposed career break.
In readiness, she had already advertised for a new assistant to be trained up to take over during her absence.

She was walking through the back door of the ballroom when she heard a woman calling Janine's name.

'Calisto…' Janine was saying in a rather strained welcome; the party planner had confided to Billie that Calisto
kept on changing her mind about what she wanted.

Billie spun around and glanced back apprehensively
over her shoulder. Calisto was casually turned out in a
red dress, a black leather jacket and high-heeled sandals.
Even at a glance the Greek woman was a striking beauty
with a magnificent blonde mane of hair and amazingly
long legs. Billie had only to think of those incredible
legs wrapped round Alexei's lean bronzed body to feel
sick and she backed away from the door before she
could be seen and walked hurriedly away. Once again
she had avoided a face-to-face meeting with Alexei's
fiancée. She had twice sidestepped encounters on the
yacht. Indeed, since Calisto's appearance on the scene,
Billie had stayed very much in the background of
Alexei's life and he had yet to bring Calisto back to
Speros for a visit. But then, the happy couple were both
very busy people who spent a lot of time on board *Sea
Queen*. Calisto, whose once stalled career had taken off
again on the strength of her new high profile with Alexei

and his A-list friends, was currently accepting modelling assignments across the globe.

Billie had arranged to spend the weekend with Hilary. Her aunt's husband—John—had passed away a month earlier and although Billie had flown over to the UK to attend the funeral she had not been able to stay on. But in spite of the open invitation to all his personal staff she had no intention of attending Alexei's family party. She was jealous and hurting inside and no matter how hard she fought not to feel and think that way she was failing.

'I've decided that I'm coming to Greece,' Hilary informed her niece. 'Once your baby's born, I'll put this house up for rent so that I have somewhere to come back to if I want to.'

Billie hugged her aunt. 'It'll make such a difference to my life and to the baby's. I just hope you're not only doing this for my sake.'

'Of course I'm not. I'm planning to write a book on King Henry IV and the House of Lancaster. Ever since university I've wanted to do it. I'll be able to do my research over the next few months with the help of the Internet,' the older woman told her with an enthusiasm that Billie hadn't seen her show in years.

'I'll be able to help you,' Billie added. 'I won't have much else to do while I'm getting through the rest of my pregnancy.'

But that prospect seemed a blessing once she saw a photo of Calisto in the fabulous ball gown she had worn for the party in the next day's newspaper. In every way Alexei was fulfilling his destiny. His family expected him to marry a woman as large as life as he was himself and Calisto, with her beauty, fame and connections, certainly fitted the bill. Billie felt another crack form in her breaking heart. She was beginning to marvel that she had ended up in bed with Alexei in the first place. That could surely only have happened because he was drunk and grieving, which was neither a comforting nor ego-boosting suspicion for her to hold.

Two weeks later, Billie was in Milan with Alexei when she broached the subject of her career break over the working lunch they were sharing.

Alexei glanced up to study her with frowning force. Her burnished copper streaked hair glinting in the sunshine, she tilted her heart-shaped face back and looked back at him with wide wary eyes as green as limes. 'Surely this is very sudden?' he queried. 'Where has this idea come from?'

'I've been thinking about it for a while. I'd like to spend some time back in England with my aunt. She could do with the support.'

'She lost her husband recently,' Alexei recalled, surprising Billie. 'Well, I have every sympathy, but I'm not prepared to tolerate some idiot trying to do your job for the next six months—'

'For a minimum of *eight* months,' Billie corrected before he could contrive to try and bargain down the duration of her absence. 'I need a break, Alexei...I really do *need* the break.'

'I don't understand why.'

'I would come back to work refreshed.'

From below lush black lashes that any woman would

have killed to possess, Alexei looked her over with keen bronze-coloured eyes of enquiry. He didn't think she looked in need of refreshment, although he was prepared to admit that she had got a little too thin in recent months, so that her clothes seemed to have become too big for her slight frame. He sensed that something was being concealed from him. 'What's really wrong?'

Her gaze took on an evasive slant. 'I just want a break and…' in a nervous flicker of motion her tongue crept out to moisten her dry lips as she braced herself to tell her first lie '…my aunt is pregnant and alone and she could do with my support.'

Alexei watched stinging colour warm her cheeks and wondered why she was blushing. Perhaps it was not the late husband's posthumous baby but the result of a fling with someone else since. He suppressed a sigh: Billie to the rescue. That made perfect sense to him. His wide sensual mouth flattened. 'I don't want you to take a break now. I consider you a vital member of my staff.'

'You've met Olympia. I'm training her to take my place.'

'Olympia skulks behind doors when I'm around. That isn't promising—'

'But that's better than a young woman who continually throws herself in your path,' Billie pointed out, well aware of how often that desire afflicted women in his radius and of how exasperating he found such behaviour. Yet she had never had the heart to judge a single one of those women when she herself had always been far too susceptible to Alexei's charisma.

'I can tell you now that Olympia won't cut it,' Alexei told her very drily.

Billie tilted her chin. 'She'll have to because I need you to agree to this career break.'

'I'll consider it.' Alexei's rich dark drawl carried more than a touch of ice. 'But why don't you consider basing yourself in my London headquarters for eight months instead? That would be a more sensible option and it would still give you a change of scene and new colleagues.'

Unprepared for that very reasonable suggestion, Billie stiffened in dismay. 'I would really rather have a complete break from my current employment.'

Alexei made her wait for a week for a final answer. She had thought she might have to remind him and her nerves suffered while she waited; if he refused she would have to hand in her resignation. He called her into his office shortly before he was due to fly out to Paris for the weekend. She entered the room, stiff-backed as she tried to shrink inside her jacket, lest the fabric fall revealingly against the small swelling mound of her stomach.

'I'm not in agreement with this career break as you call it,' Alexei informed her without hesitation, his dark golden eyes grim and cool. 'It'll be a nuisance, but you've worked well for me for some years now and I am conscious of that. When do you want to go on leave?'

'At the end of the month,' she told him, weak with relief but taut with guilt at the tangle of deception that she was embarking on.

But she could not see a choice. Although an engagement had yet to be announced, Calisto was already said to be consulting wedding planners. Billie could only hope that the marriage would take place before her return. The passage of time, she told herself urgently, would cure her of sleepless nights and the erotic longings that embarrassed the hell out of her.

She wasn't herself any more. It was as if Alexei had picked her up and shaken her so that nothing inside her was in the right place any more. She was at the mercy of her hormones, of passionate crying jags and, sometimes, wild crazy thoughts and hopes. Distance would cure her, give her the chance to get over him, she told herself fiercely, because if she was planning to return to work for Alexei, she needed to grow a tougher skin.

'You and my sister are thick as thieves at present,' Lauren remarked when her daughter came to say her goodbyes, her burgeoning tummy carefully concealed below a loose T-shirt and a canvas jacket. 'When are you planning to tell me what's really going on?'

Billie ducked the question and gave Lauren a guilty hug, wondering how she would ever face telling the truth to her mother, who was sure to have some very cutting comments to make when the time came. But all that really mattered to her at that moment was that, step by step, her plan was working…

Eight months later, as she'd promised, Billie made her return to Speros. She stood on the ferry with Hilary and Nikolos, who had become known as Nicky within days of his birth. She pointed out landmarks on the island to Hilary, who was glowing with enthusiasm by her side. With her short blonde hair tousling in the breeze, her aunt's brown eyes were alight with curiosity and excitement.

'So that's your house…my new home,' Hilary breathed, straining to see the small dwelling to the right of the vast Drakos compound. 'And that massive yacht out there is *Sea Queen*? I had no idea the yacht was as big as a cruise liner.'

'You'll be able to come on aboard and tour the yacht on St George's Day,' Billie commented. 'The whole island takes a holiday for the festival of *Agios Georgios* and although it's the celebration of the saint that the village church is dedicated to, there's also a lot of fun with bonfires on the beach and loads of food and drink.'

'I'm looking forward to it. I remember you talking about it a couple of years ago,' Hilary admitted. 'Isn't it typical that Nicky has finally fallen asleep?'

Billie gave her infant son a rueful look. That was Hilary's polite way of saying that Nicky had been a little horror for most of the journey from London, evidently disliking the changes in his usual routine. He had cried for most of the flight and had refused to settle in between times. Offers of bottles, changes and cuddles had made no impression on his general dissatisfaction with life.

'I can't wait to see my house. The photos Damon emailed only whet my appetite.' Billie's arm was aching and she shifted Nicky to her other shoulder, where he continued to doze, his little breathy snuffles sounding in her ear. He was a surprisingly heavy bundle for a baby of only three months old. She stroked his back, wondering how she would bear working for hours away from him every day but knowing that, like millions of other working mothers, she had no choice.

Lauren greeted them at the harbour and made a beeline for the baby, who was now in Hilary's arms. 'So this is my…nephew,' she exclaimed, and it seemed to her daughter that there was a deliberate hesitation over that designation. 'My goodness, he looks older than three months and he's rather Mediterranean in his colouring, isn't he? I wonder who he got all that black hair from—'

'Don't exaggerate, Lauren. He's not a baby werewolf.' Hilary reclaimed the sleepy baby from her sister and clambered after Billie into the village taxi.

'What colour are his eyes?'

'Brown.' Billie avoided the hard stare her mother was subjecting her to from the front passenger seat.

Mercifully the new house took over as the topic of conversation. Billie had had furniture and household effects ready in storage before she even left the island and Lauren and Alexei's housekeeper, Anatalya, had worked together to find a place for everything. The two women had done a great job, but Billie realised that the furnishings looked sparse, particularly when the wood and tiled floors and white walls were bare of any adornment.

'It's so light and bright!' Hilary carolled, walking out onto the terrace where Billie was already admiring the wonderful panoramic view of the bay. 'It's amazing, a fabulous house and so spacious. Should we put Nicky down for a nap?'

'You're his mother, darling. Surely that should be your decision,' Lauren interposed with suggestive bite.

'He's the most beautiful baby!' Anatalya exclaimed in admiration, bridging the awkward moment between the three women related by blood.

Nicky was settled in his nursery where a musical mobile was switched on for his entertainment. He watched it with wide unblinking dark eyes and then his little face creased and he began to grizzle and complain.

'I think the mobile is irritating him,' Hilary opined.

Billie switched it off.

'So the baby rules the roost,' Lauren remarked from the doorway. 'Is it, by any chance…a Drakos baby?'

'Shush!' Billie hissed at her mother in shock. 'Don't even breathe an insinuation like that!'

'I worked it out a long time ago. That's why he gave you the building plot next door—'

'Billie!' Anatalya called.

Relieved by the excuse to move, Billie slid past her mother to answer the older woman, whose plump smiling face was set in an unusual expression of discomfiture as she returned a mobile phone to her pocket. 'What is it?'

'Thespinis Calisto has just phoned me to say that she would like to see you immediately.'

Billie swallowed hard. As Lauren broke into rude comment Billie gave her mother's arm a warning squeeze. 'She's probably going to be my boss's wife, so although I don't start back to work officially until tomorrow I had better show willing.'

'I'll soon find my way around. Nicky and we'll be fine,' Hilary declared.

Billie got into Anatalya's beat-up old car. Alexei was

heading home from Australia and not due back until later that night. And here Billie was finally heading for the meeting she had managed to avoid for months. 'Do I address her now as Miss Calisto or Mrs Bethune?' she asked the older woman.

'She told us all to call her the first. We all find her difficult,' the housekeeper admitted heavily. 'She has new ideas about the way we do everything at the villa.'

'Well, that's to be expected,' Billie quipped with determined good cheer. *What can't be cured must be endured* had become her personal mantra in recent months.

Calisto elected to see her in Alexei's office. She was still gorgeous, all blonde hair, white teeth and long legs displayed to advantage by a fluorescent pink dress.

'So you're Billie,' the statuesque blonde pronounced, treating her husband's employee to a head-to-toe unimpressed appraisal, her lips curling with scorn. 'There's loads of things going wrong at Alexei's properties because you've taken too much time off.'

'I'm sorry. It's unfortunate that my replacement didn't work out.'

'You're very lucky to have a job to come back to.' Calisto lifted a sheet of paper and extended it in a regal gesture of command. A whiff of her expensive perfume engulfed Billie. 'I've made a list of the most important things you need to take care of. I hope you're planning on working late tonight.'

'No, not tonight. I've been travelling since early this morning. But I'll make a start now,' Billie declared equably, glancing down at the entries on the paper. It was not a factual list of tasks, rather a long list of complaints that appeared to range from a poorly maintained swimming pool to impertinent domestic staff and finally colour and furnishing schemes that Alexei's consort wanted changed. 'I'll soon get it all sorted out.'

'See that you do. Alexei likes things to run like clockwork. He has no patience for cock-ups and neither do I. He says you're very efficient and this is your chance to prove it.'

Billie nodded and went to the door that led through to her own office space.

'I believe you organise things here for *Agios Georgios* day,' Calisto remarked in sudden addition. 'Do you think you could cancel the open house reception here at the villa?'

'It became a tradition when Alexei's father was a boy.'

'Yes, well, we're the new generation and I like my privacy. I don't fancy the local fisherfolk marching through our home. Make sure it doesn't happen.'

Billie said nothing, for it was not within her power to make such a decision. She suspected that Alexei, who had great respect for island tradition and hospitality, would insist that the usual arrangements went ahead.

That night she slept in her new house for the first time, the smell of fresh paint and new furniture in her nostrils. She wakened very early, fed and dressed Nicky, who was squirming with morning liveliness in his cot, and decided to go for a swim before getting ready for work. Hilary didn't fancy swimming at that hour and prepared breakfast to eat out on the terrace.

The beach on the other side of the narrow coastal road was a stretch of pale golden sand. Billie shed her towelling robe on a rock and waded into the water, shivering at the chill of it. The water was colder than she had expected and she realised that she had been spoiled by the temperature of the Drakos swimming pool. After a vigorous swim to warm up, she had walked back up the beach before she realised that she was no longer alone.

Alexei, casually dressed in faded jeans and a black sweater, and with dark stubble outlining his stubborn jaw line and wilful sensual mouth, strode across the sand towards her. 'I saw you from the villa,' he drawled with a smile. 'England has made you hardier. That water is icy.'

'A little colder than I expected,' Billie conceded, her full attention welded to him for their first meeting in eight interminable months. And he did not disappoint her. Even fresh and unshaven from Calisto's bed, a thought that sent a sharp slicing arrow of pain through her, Alexei looked stunningly handsome. Furthermore, his aura of raw energy and white-hot sexuality hit her like a force field. A tingle of urgent heat speared between her legs and she came to a sudden halt, trying not to shiver from awareness as much as from cold.

Long before he had reached her, Alexei had noted the full lush silhouette of her breasts and hips in the swimsuit. Had her curves always been that pronounced, that spectacular? Surely not? With her Titian hair trailing in wet dark red ribbons against her white skin and her nipples protruding through the clinging fabric, she was intensely sexy, and as his body reacted his jeans grew tight. He didn't fight it either, but he was frantically striving to work out how she could have that effect on him when her hair was in a mess, she wore no make-up and her costume was as old as the hills.

Self-consciousness made Billie hurry on until she could grasp her robe, pull it on and turn back to him. Although she had lost almost all her pregnancy weight, her breasts had gained a cup size and her stomach, no matter how hard she sucked it in, now had a slightly rounded curve.

'You're never getting a career break again,' Alexei warned her. 'Things I took for granted have gone haywire without you.'

'I'll hit the ground running,' she promised him.

'Bring your aunt up to join Calisto and me for dinner tonight,' he told her. 'What do you think of your house?'

'It's wonderful.'

'Damon actually pulled it off.'

Her eyes gleamed emerald. 'With a lot of interference from you.'

'He's back with his wife and kids where he belongs,' Alexei told her. 'I was on target there, wasn't I?'

'I'm glad they're back together.' Billie refused to rise to the bait he offered. 'I'd better get back home or I'll be late.'

'I believe you have an understanding employer.' Brilliant bronzed eyes held hers for a long moment and her tummy performed a somersault. 'I noticed your absence, *moraki mou*.'

Without warning, hot burning tears pricked the backs of her eyes. With a forced smile and a clumsy wave, she sped off back home. She spent a busy day working and asked Anatalya's daughter to babysit for her that evening.

Hilary was very impressed by the dinner invitation and fussed over what she wore. 'We're keeping his son from him. I can't afford to like him,' she said uneasily.

'It's a lovely welcome to the island for you.'

'I'm dying to see Alexei's home, and the gilded lifestyle of a billionaire!' Hilary rolled her eyes with humour.

It was fortunate that Hilary was in an upbeat mood, for Calisto could not have made her dislike of the occasion and the guests more obvious. Alexei drew out Hilary's intention of writing a book about King Henry IV, while Calisto sighed, wrinkled her classic nose and yawned with boredom before rising to put on music at a volume that made it difficult to continue the conversation. Billie saw Alexei glance at his fiancée and knew he was annoyed. Whatever faults he had, generosity and courtesy towards guests were sacrosanct to him. His shrewd gaze rested on Billie for an instant and she reddened fiercely, hoping he couldn't sense her uncharitable thoughts.

'I'm glad I got the chance to meet Calisto,' Hilary told her niece late that evening. 'How can Alexei be in love with a woman like that? He's a clever, cultivated man and she's a spoiled brat with no manners and, I suspect, pretty dim—'

'Let's face it, you're biased. She *is* a very beautiful woman.'

'That won't be enough to sustain a durable relationship.'

'Alexei is no fool. He must see something in Calisto that we don't,' Billie responded heavily.

'Maybe you should come clean with him about Nicky—'

'No! Why are you saying that now?' Billie demanded in dismay.

'You should tell him before he gets married to another woman. It wouldn't be fair to either him or his wife if you dumped the news on them afterwards.'

'He's not planning on getting married yet.' That question settled, Billie cuddled Nicky, her son a drowsy and sweet-smelling weight in her protective arms. He was adorable. She could not imagine Alexei as a father, only as a lover, and that was a discomfiting realisation. She tucked her child back into his cot and wished him goodnight.

The minute she told Alexei that Nicky was his, her whole life would change, because she would hardly be able to continue in her job. In addition, what relationship she did have with Alexei would be destroyed. An inner chill pierced her deep at that prospect. Shorn of the memory of their sexual encounter, he wouldn't believe her story. Initially she would just seem like another one of the gold-digging women who had tried to entrap a share of his huge wealth.

No, Billie decided doggedly, having gone to such lengths to conceal her secret, she would be very careful to pick the optimum moment to tell Alexei the truth. When that precise moment came, her sixth sense would tell her…

CHAPTER NINE

Two weeks later, the celebration of *Agios Giorgios* began with a parade to the little church down by the harbour and a celebratory service, which Alexei and most of his staff attended.

A buffet lunch for all followed at the Drakos villa, where games and amusements were laid on for the island children. As a former teacher Hilary was a great help with organising fun activities to keep the children occupied. At Calisto's request, Billie had made arrangements for a private lunch for Alexei, Calisto and their house guests, but Alexei excused himself from the meal in the isolation of the separate dining room and attended the villagers' buffet instead. That there was tension between him and his girlfriend was obvious to everyone.

Billie watched him circulate. He cut a flawless figure in a superbly tailored silk-blend grey suit while his air of command and self-assurance left no one in any doubt of his elite status. But he mixed with the villagers at a much more comfortable level than his late father,

Constantine, ever had. He kicked a stray ball back to the boys playing football on his immaculate lawns.

'Tell Alexei I want to speak to him,' Calisto instructed Billie, who was watching over events from the shade of the terrace.

Billie glanced at the beautiful blonde, gloriously if impractically clad in a pure white dress that was low of neck and very short of skirt. Her mouth compressing into an apologetic line as she approached Alexei, she did as she was asked.

His lean, darkly handsome features took on a forbidding aspect and Billie marvelled at Calisto's lack of savvy about the man she was hoping to marry. In certain moods, Alexei needed lots of space. A woman who clung or demanded more attention at that point could only infuriate him. And summoning him through a third party, who was also an employee, was an absolute no-no.

'Calisto and I will go out to *Sea Queen* now,' Alexei imparted. 'I'll leave you to oversee the transfer of our visitors.'

Billie nodded, sensing the anger he was controlling, grateful she was not the target. Alexei could be so unpredictable and volatile and she sensed that Calisto had very little idea of how his mind worked. All the seething passion and power of Alexei's strong personality could suddenly ignite like a volcano and—like lava—he would burn everything he came into contact with.

When she arrived on the yacht with Hilary and Nicky, Captain McGregor got talking to her aunt and offered to act as her escort for a personal tour of the luxurious vessel. It was fortunate that Billie was able to leave

Hilary in good hands because, with Calisto nowhere to be seen, Billie was forced to act as hostess and greet and organise the arrivals.

Much later that afternoon, Billie found Alexei squatting down on deck in an effort to calm a lost little boy who was crying noisily. She went to his assistance, lifting the child to comfort him and recognising him as the son of the island nurse. 'He needs his mum. I'll go and find her,' she told Alexei softly. 'He's probably over-tired and high on sugar from all those treats you laid on for the kids.'

'It's only once a year.' Straightening again, Alexei gazed down at his PA with hooded dark-as-ebony eyes that were unusually serious and contained no glint of gold. The toddler was now clinging trustingly to Billie with chocolate-stained fingers and sucking his thumb. '*Efharisto, moraki mou.* You like children, don't you?'

Billie paled. 'Very much.'

His darkly handsome face shadowed and hardened as though that response was the wrong one and, without another word, he inclined his proud dark head in acknowledgement and left her to it. She restored the toddler to his grateful mother, who had assumed her youngest child was being looked after by his older siblings. When it was time for all the locals to return to dry land, Calisto finally put in a grudging appearance on deck. Her once-pristine white designer dress now bore stains and it looked as though an attempt to clean it had enjoyed little success. There was quite a breeze and seeing Billie—who had left her jacket on shore—shiver, Alexei had a word with one of the stewards, who went

off and returned with a soft cream-coloured pashmina.
Alexei draped the wrap round Billie's bare shoulders.

Taken aback by that considerate gesture and mortified by the angrily accusing stare she was receiving
from Calisto, who seemed to be in a particularly bad
mood, Billie busied herself with ensuring the guests
enjoyed a smooth departure. She was hurrying off to
look for Hilary and Nicky when Calisto cornered her as
she walked past the main salon. 'Come in, I need to
speak to you.'

Billie fell still, her anxious green eyes flying to the
set of Calisto's petulant face. 'How can I help?'

'By keeping your distance from Alexei. For such a
plain little thing, you're very good at attracting attention
to yourself. You're far too familiar with Alexei and I won't
tolerate you flirting with him right under my nose—'

Rigid with resentment, Billie lifted her chin. 'I
don't behave like that. Now if you don't mind, I have
to find my aunt—'

'I *do* mind. How dare you walk away from me when
I haven't finished speaking to you?' Calisto launched at
her an octave higher and several notches louder in
volume. Billie decided that flight would be wiser than
an argument with her employer's enraged partner.

'Hilary and her son are out on deck with McGregor,
Billie. Go and join her. Thank you for your assistance
today,' Alexei interposed from behind Calisto, his lean,
strong face grim. 'I will deal with this.'

Relieved by his intervention, even though she feared
that it would win her Calisto's undying hatred, Billie did
as she was told. Behind her she heard Calisto raise her

voice again and breathed in deep. If only Alexei hadn't made that gesture with the wrap! But Alexei was like that, prone to little random acts of thoughtfulness that people didn't expect from so rich and powerful a man. There had been nothing remotely intimate or flirtatious in his behaviour. A little old lady could just as easily have been the recipient of his consideration. Billie pressed clammy hands to her hot cheeks. No, indeed, Calisto had misunderstood what she saw. When Alexei got truly intimate with a woman, he crossed boundaries with the speed, power and high visibility of a champion racehorse.

Hilary looked unusually distracted when they finally got back to the house after the bonfires and the firework display on the beach. Billie reclaimed Nicky and urged her aunt to put her feet up for what little remained of the evening.

'I'm fine...I do like Stuart,' the blonde woman confided.

'Stuart?' Billie hadn't a clue who the other woman was referring to.

'Stuart McGregor, the captain of Alexei's yacht. He's a lovely man, quiet but very well read,' Hilary declared.

'I don't know him very well,' Billie admitted. 'The yacht crew don't mix much with Alexei's other employees, but I'm glad you enjoyed yourself.'

When Billie started work the next morning at the villa, she was surprised to discover that Alexei had already flown to New York.

'Did Calisto accompany him?' Billie asked the housekeeper.

'No. She flew back to Athens last night.' Anatalya

came closer and lowered her voice. 'I think Mr Alexei has broken up with her. I heard her shouting and when she left she took everything she owned with her.'

'Probably just a tiff,' Billie suggested, less prone to jumping to conclusions than the older woman. 'They've been together for almost a year now.'

But Anatalya was right on target: the gossip columns and the celebrity magazines confirmed that the relationship was over later that week. On the cover of one glossy journal there was a photo of Alexei and Calisto together with a jagged line like lightning separating them. Alexei had refused to comment when asked why, but Calisto had given a couple of interviews and implied that Alexei's reputation and party lifestyle had given her pause for thought.

At the start of the following week, Alexei phoned Billie and told her that he needed her to fly over to his English country house. He was staging an important business meeting there and he wanted Billie to ensure that all the arrangements flowed smoothly.

'We knew you'd have to travel. It's part of your job,' Hilary reminded her niece as Billie held her baby son close and wondered anxiously how long she would be away from him. Secrecy was all very well, she began to appreciate, but there were definite drawbacks. Had Alexei known that she was a mother he would never have expected her to leave her child for days on end.

'When he left you behind here on the island, you worried that your role was being reduced,' Hilary added. 'So, you can't complain now.'

Billie breathed in the sweet familiar scent of her baby

and hugged him, loving the weight and feel of his little trusting body in her arms. 'I just don't want to leave him.'

'You can phone every hour of the day and I'll put him on the webcam,' her aunt promised sympathetically.

It was well over a year since Billie had visited Hazlehurst Manor in Kent. Although she had planned to hire a car at the airport, Alexei had sent a vehicle to pick her up. From the instant the car turned up the long stately driveway to the imposing Georgian pile, her eyes were anxiously scanning from left to right for maintenance issues that would require attention. But the verges were neat, the parkland picturesque and what she could see of the manicured hedges suggested that the gardens were just as well groomed. She was greeted by the manor's highly efficient housekeeper and taken straight off for a tour.

A suite on the ground floor, complete with a facility for tea and coffee, had already been set up as a conference centre. The bedrooms were as well prepared for occupation as any in an exclusive hotel. Billie was impressed and said so—on the accommodation front there was nothing left for her to do. Alexei arrived in a helicopter late the following morning while Billie was going over some estimates for renovations to the kitchen quarters. He strode into the office where she was working, his black hair blown back from his lean bronzed features, an unexpected smile tilting his passionate and wilful mouth. It lightened the often forbidding aspect that had long characterised the Drakos reputation in the business world.

'For the first time, I feel you're back where you

belong…ensuring everything runs like clockwork.'
Alexei studied her closely, wishing her vibrant hair were
loose instead of tightly confined and mentally reclothing
her in garments more appealing than the black pin-
stripe skirt suit she wore. He would like those little
fingernails painted too. His sense of anticipation spiked,
his body reacting with hot sexuality to the concept of
Billie's lush little body clad in silk and lace lingerie, and
for the first time there was no guilt, no sense that such
thoughts, images and reactions were inappropriate
where she was concerned. And why was that so? His in-
tentions were wholly honourable for possibly the first
time in his life.

Dry-mouthed at the full spectacular masculine effect
of Alexei Drakos up close, Billie scrambled upright,
her heart drumming out a disturbing tattoo behind her
breastbone. 'Everything was done before I arrived. The
housekeeper here is a gem.'

His beautiful smile broadened, showing a flash of
strong white teeth. 'Generous to others as well. You
have many sterling qualities, Billie. My guests arrive
this afternoon and I would like you to act as my hostess
while they're here.'

Billie inclined her bright head in acknowledgement.

'But as I imagine you didn't pack for that eventuality
I ordered some clothes for you.'

Her green eyes widened. 'You ordered clothes for
me?' she queried in surprise.

'I don't want you running round dressed in a business
suit for the next forty-eight hours, *moraki mou*.'

In receipt of the full stunning burn of his dark golden

eyes welded to her, Billie tensed as sexual awareness prickled over her entire skin surface and made heat lick in private places. 'I thought we had agreed that you wouldn't call me something like that…'

Alexei laughed out loud. It occurred to her that for a man whose recent romance had gone down in flames of invasive publicity he was in a remarkably good mood. 'No, you objected, but I made no such agreement. I'll call you what I like.'

That arrogant assurance was vintage Drakos and ironically eased Billie's tension a little, since up until that instant he had been behaving in an unfamiliar manner. With the experience of long acquaintance guiding her, she moved on to more business-orientated matters. 'I've been going over the figures for the proposed renovations here and I'll have to discuss the budget with you before I can establish—'

'No, no work for the moment. Go and put on one of the new outfits and join me for lunch,' Alexei instructed, determined to lift their relationship right out of the usual business mode.

'But your guests won't arrive until later.'

'Is there some particular reason why you need to argue with me today?' Alexei enquired in a drawl as smooth and acerbic as a diamond cutter.

Billie parted her lips and then closed them again. It annoyed her that she didn't know why he was behaving as he was. Buying her clothes, for example: what was that all about? Years ago, when he had helped equip her for her new job with him, he had known she didn't have the money to purchase smart suits and there had been good reason for his generosity. But why now, all of a sudden, should it matter to him what she wore? Was he suggesting that she was dressing badly again? Trying to smarten her up? Embarrassment claimed her until she went up to her room where she discovered that a staggering array of designer clothes awaited her attention. Not one of those outfits impressed her as being suitable for work wear. The collection of lingerie took her very much aback as it was far too intimate a purchase for him to have made on her behalf. She assumed he had instructed some personal shopper and that the lingerie was a mistake.

Mistake or otherwise, however, Billie was intrigued by the exquisite undergarments and finally succumbed to the temptation of seeing herself garbed in pastel-blue silk lingerie of the most frivolous and revealing kind. She picked a devastatingly simple royal-blue dress with a draped neckline and a short-sleeved jacket from a famous designer and put them on, posing in high strappy heels and barely recognising her reflection. She let her hair down, ran a comb through the thick tangle of coppery red strands that tumbled round her face and smiled. So *this* was how feeling you looked your best felt! She knew she should take the outfit off, go back downstairs and tell him that she could not possibly accept a virtual new wardrobe from him. Shamingly, however, and her cheeks reddened at this awareness, she badly wanted him to see her clad in her fine feathers first.

Alexei's black-lashed gaze whipped over Billie's slender elegant figure with considerable satisfaction when she reappeared. 'You don't look like my PA any more.'

'And that's not right,' Billie pointed out earnestly.

'It is if you're in line for a promotion…a major kind of promotion,' Alexei framed with teasing precision. 'I've thought a lot about you since I ditched Calisto and I have reached a fascinating conclusion. You're the shining example of the sort of woman I want to marry.'

Her eyes wide with bemusement at that far-reaching statement, Billie breathed weakly, 'I suppose I should say thanks for the compliment.'

'I know you inside out. You know and understand me,' Alexei asserted with formidable cool as he guided her into the dining room with a light hand resting to her spine. 'You have all the qualities I admire: honesty, self-respect, courage and kindness. The people who surround me like and respect you as well.'

'I just work for you. You're making me uncomfortable,' Billie reproved, shaking out her napkin and taking a seat opposite him with two high spots of colour burnishing her cheeks.

'Don't tell fibs,' Alexei derided. 'There's a strong sexual attraction between us and there always has been.'

Her face felt so hot that she honestly feared her skin was on fire. 'I don't understand what all this is about or why you're talking to me like this—'

'Then don't interrupt, and listen,' Alexei cut in with withering bite. 'I'm not a romantic man. I never have been. I never will be. Calisto was a major mistake and I'm grateful to have appreciated that fact before I put a wedding ring on her finger. But that fiasco did make me think about what's important in a life partnership, what I want from a woman and what that woman might expect from me.'

'Well, that's very sensible but just at present I imagine you're feeling rather anti-women and not thinking quite as clearly as you believe you are.'

His lean, darkly handsome face tensed and darkened, his eyes narrowing with hauteur. 'That's where you're wrong. I have never been so sure of a decision before. To be frank, I don't spend much time thinking about my relationships with women.'

'I know,' Billie agreed feelingly, thinking of some of the appalling mismatches that had featured in his past love life.

'You know the worst I'm capable of.'

Billie wondered why he was talking to her in such an unusually intimate vein and her brow stayed indented in a frown. She was tense and uneasy.

'Let me have my say first,' Alexei urged her as if he perfectly understood her bewilderment. 'I'm bored of casual sex.'

'Well, it took you a long time to get to that point, but that you did get there finally is in your favour,' Billie informed him cheerfully to cover up her embarrassment at that blunt admission.

'If you don't keep quiet for five minutes, I may well strangle you!' Alexei groaned in exasperation. 'Right now, I'm ready to settle down and get married and *you* are the only woman I can see in that role. I want to marry you.'

Billie froze in shock and stared at him, unable to believe that he could mean what he had just said. The silence that followed came down like a crushing weight on her nerves.

'I have more faith in you than in any woman I've ever

met and our relationship is not based purely on sex, or on your love of my wealth. I'm convinced that the talents that have made you a dependable and trustworthy employee will make you an even better wife,' he concluded grimly. 'So, I'm asking you the question I never got as far as asking Calisto… Will you be my wife?'

'You can't ask me that only a week after you've broken up with another woman!' Billie suddenly launched at him in helpless condemnation. 'You're on the rebound. You don't know what you're doing!'

'Of course I know what I'm doing,' Alexei fielded in dry exasperation.

Although he was offering Billie what she had most wanted in the world for several years, it was in terms that she found horribly humiliating. In addition, words like 'dependable' and 'trustworthy' tore her up inside when she recalled the game of deception she had become engaged in over a year earlier—and in which she was still up to her throat. He probably thought he knew the worst of her as well, but he *didn't*. Nor was his proposal of marriage of the type that had ever featured in her dreams. He didn't love her. He was simply fed up dating and, having been disappointed by Calisto, he had decided to settle for a woman he believed he knew inside out. A sensible woman with a good work ethic who knew him well: Billie. It was a very logical decision and very much Alexei who, for all his passion and volatility, was now focusing his remarkably practical and shrewd business brain on the institution of matrimony. Was he choosing her as the low-risk, low-maintenance option in the bridal stakes?

'You haven't even explained why you broke up with Calisto yet.'

His aggressive jaw line squared. 'Nor do I intend to. Why pick over the past? There is no comparison between you and Calisto. Our marriage would have much firmer foundations.'

Of course there could be no comparison between ordinary Billie Foster and the gorgeous model, Calisto Bethune. A shard of bitter anger and pain pierced Billie at his unhesitating candour. Alexei, Billie suspected, thought that there would be no ups and downs with *her*, that she would be so quiet and eager to please that waves would be non-existent. But he was thinking that way because he wasn't allowing for the reality that how Billie behaved as an employee would scarcely be the same as she behaved as a wife. It burned a smoking hole in her heart that he should ask her to marry him because he respected her as a person and admired what he saw as her sterling character. How much would he respect her if he knew the truth of what she was capable of? If she told him the truth about Nicky, if she told him she had conceived his child and concealed the birth from him, he would hold her lies against her and he would no longer want to marry her.

'I don't want to talk about this any more,' Billie announced, planting her hands down on the table surface and forcing her slim body upright in a move that patently took him by surprise. 'I need to think about this.'

'Why?' Alexei thrust his chair back and sprang up. Bronzed eyes gleaming like polished metal, he gazed down into her troubled heart-shaped face and breathed in a raw growling undertone, 'What's to think about, *moraki mou*? I know you've always cared about me.'

Sparks of rage lit up inside Billie and fuelled the angry step she took back from the table. So that was the true deal, she reflected in raging pain. She was to supply the love in this sensible marriage of minds—only until now he had been too modest and polite to say so. He might not love her but he had no objection to being loved. At least he would make no objection as long as she made no demands. Indeed, Billie was under few illusions as to the exact nature of the marriage she was being offered: a matter-of-fact partnership based on mutual respect and sexual attraction.

'It's a very insulting proposal,' Billie told him flatly.

'*Insulting?*' Alexei repeated in thunderous disbelief. 'How have I insulted you?'

'Just you think about what you've said to me and then ask yourself how many women would want to marry you on those terms!' Billie flung back at him furiously as she stalked out of the room, headed straight to the front door and out into the fresh air.

Her hasty steps only slowing as she reached the concealment of the garden hidden behind manicured hedges, Billie pressed the heel of her hand to the thunderous pounding at her temples and trembled at the force of the emotions she was striving to rein back. A jumble of mortifying phrases were still assailing her and making her cringe. *A major kind of promotion. Dependable? Trustworthy? I'm bored of casual sex. No comparison between you and Calisto.* She was the safe alternative to his capricious ex-fiancée, as cosy and

insipid as hot milk when compared to such a spicy
cocktail. Calisto's high jinks and the memory of his
father's three very costly divorces had made Alexei
cautious in the matrimonial stakes. He didn't want a
wife who would rock the boat with emotional outbursts
and petulant demands. He wanted a wife who would do
as she was told just like an employee, a wife who was
grateful enough for her position to let him live his life
without interference. No, such a marriage was not the
stuff of which dreams were made and it never would be.

Billie sank down heavily on a bench overlooking a
still circular pond that reflected the smooth green sur-
rounding lawn. Only in a fantastic dream would Alexei
Drakos ever have proposed to her in any other terms, she
told herself in exasperation. Of course he wasn't in love
with her. She wasn't drop-dead gorgeous or even a sen-
sational challenge to his masculinity. She was his social
secretary who had long been in love with him.

And just how long had he been aware of that crucial
fact? Her face stung with shamed heat. No doubt she had
betrayed her true feelings for him long ago, because he
was a man who knew and understood women all too
well. Never by word or by gesture, however, had he
revealed his knowledge until now when, in the act of
honouring her with a marriage proposal, he had joined
up all the dots to point out how well she would suit him.

She had no doubt whatsoever that he saw his
proposal as an honour he conferred upon her. After
all, what did she have to offer a young, handsome billionaire but her very ordinariness? Yet, astonishingly,
that ordinariness was suddenly what he had decided

would best suit his requirements. A humble, grateful, loving wife would, of course, be far easier to live with than a diva like Calisto Bethune. You had to hand it to Alexei—even marriage had to be one hundred per cent on *his* terms. For, really, what would be in it for her?

Billie breathed in deep as she reached the crux of the matter. It was all very well storming off in a passion of hurt pride and wounded feelings, but was she really going to say no to her one and only chance to become Alexei's wife? So, as proposals went, it had been a patronizing, humiliating insult. But he had been honest with her about his expectations and he had evidently never got as far as actually asking Calisto to marry him, which could only please Billie. But then had Alexei even loved Calisto? Indeed had he *ever* been in love? Billie had never even heard him mention the word. Alexei had always had a detached quality with women.

Billie thought about Alexei's own background and acknowledged that it was scarcely the stuff of dreams either. His parents' shotgun marriage had been, on the face of it, a successful relationship, but Natasha Drakos had deferred very much to her older husband in every field. It had been a very traditional and conservative Greek union in which Constantine had travelled while Natasha had stayed home, dutifully fulfilling the roles of wife, hostess and mother. That kind of controlled unemotional relationship, Billie finally registered, was the blueprint that Alexei—whether he realised it or not—was applying to his own marital plans.

'The big flare-up and walk out isn't like you,' Alexei

breathed coolly from several feet away. 'I expected you to be sensible.'

For a male who knew women, he was being appallingly tactless. Billie lifted her lashes to look at him, smitten to the heart by his dark male beauty. 'I am being sensible. I'm thinking over what you said.'

'What is there to think over?' Alexei fielded drily.

Billie tilted her chin, green eyes sparkling. 'You don't love me. You'll be difficult to live with. You'll always want your own way. You may not be faithful. I think there's plenty there for me to think about.'

As she spoke dark blood had coloured his high cheekbones and his sleek bone structure tightened defensively below his tawny skin. She knew it was a struggle for him not to snap back at her and cut her off at the knees for her cheek. 'I'll give you my answer tomorrow.'

'I trust you to make the right decision,' Alexei retorted.

He trusted her! Oh, dear heaven, Billie thought in a maelstrom of anguish at his careless assurance, he *trusted* her! Yet if he knew that he had a son called Nicky, his trust would be destroyed. That awareness was like a stiletto knife in her heart, yet she was convinced that she dared not come clean with him at that moment.

A lean hand closed over hers to raise her from the bench and then splayed to the curve of her hips to tilt her against his strong muscular length. Alexei lowered his handsome dark head. 'I want you—much more than you've ever appreciated, *matakia mou*.'

His lips covered hers and she literally stopped breathing, caught up in the moment of searing eroticism that pierced her body when his tongue plunged deep into the tender interior of her mouth. She shivered as if she were in the eye of a storm-force wind, hunger storming through her slight body with sudden fierce impatience, for having once tasted the heat of his passion she longed to feel it again.

The intensity of her response to a single kiss shook Alexei and aroused him even more. He backed off though, determined to take that aspect of their relationship slowly. He was convinced that he would be her first lover and was tantalised by the idea.

'As I know you're not experienced I won't expect you to share my bed until we're married,' Alexei breathed huskily. 'So, as I'm sure you will understand, I don't want to wait long for the wedding.'

Billie almost shielded her gaze with defensive lashes. He had assumed she was still a virgin, had no idea that he had already ensured that she could no longer claim such innocence. He had no fear that she might refuse his proposal either. His arrogance infuriated her.

'I might say no tomorrow,' she pointed out stiffly.

Alexei hauled her even closer and kissed her again, long and hard and sexily. His lean hands smoothed over her ribcage, tantalisingly close to the swollen sensitivity of her full breasts. Emerging breathless from that heated embrace, Billie could barely focus or breathe, never mind think and reason. The very feel of his long, lean, aroused body pushing in demand against hers paralysed her brain and ignited her to a fierce fever pitch of longing.

That night she barely slept for excitement. He didn't love her but she loved him and knew it would break her

heart to stand by while he married someone else, as he
inevitably would should she refuse him. Her heart ruled
her, even though her head warned her that the path ahead
would be twisty and stony. She joined him in his private
dining room for breakfast.

'Your answer?' Alexei enquired silkily.

'Yes, I will marry you,' Billie pronounced, watching
his wide sensual mouth curl with satisfaction. 'Are you
surprised?'

'No, as I have already said, I have enormous faith in
you, *khriso mou*,' Alexei confided, sending a sharp pang
of guilt and regret through Billie's slender body. My
gold, my treasure, he'd called her. But for how much
longer would he see her in that idealised light?

CHAPTER TEN

Two and a half weeks later, Billie studied the exquisite emerald engagement ring on her finger.

It was a slim elegant ring mounted with a deep green stone of surpassing beauty that complemented her small hand; Billie had to keep on checking it out to convince herself that she had not accidentally stepped into a dream. When she was holding onto so many secrets, how could planning her wedding feel real? First and foremost, Alexei respected her for her ability to tell the truth. Finding out that she had lied and lied again would be a very unpleasant surprise for him.

'You have to tell him about Nicky *before* you marry him,' Hilary pronounced without hesitation.

'If I do, he won't marry me,' Billie muttered feverishly.

Unmoved by that view, Hilary shook her blonde head. 'That's a risk you have to take.'

But Billie's courage had failed her on that score. Even two weeks after the proposal, wedding bells were still pealing inside her head. She finally had the magical right to hug the guy she had fallen in love with, although opportunities to do so had been few because he had hardly been around since the day he had proposed. Billie had stayed on Speros to organise the wedding while Alexei was abroad on business. Even so, her world had suddenly become a place of infinite promise and happiness, and confessing up to the deception of the year over their son, Nicky, had little appeal. Indeed her dishonesty hung over her like a giant black rain cloud that carried the threat of imminent doom.

Her face very pale, Billie murmured tautly, 'Alexei might try to take Nicky away from me.'

Hilary frowned. 'Why would he do something like that?'

'Because he'll be so angry. He's a control freak. I'll have let him down, hidden the truth from him…and he *hates* lies. An illegitimate child will also embarrass his family. He'll blame me.'

'Of course she can't tell Alexei about Nicky until she's got that wedding ring safely on her finger!' Lauren broke in, shooting her younger sister a look of angry derision that dismissed her advice. 'He's a Drakos and as slippery in the wedding stakes as a man can be. He's very wary of marriage—of course he is…his father did have four wives! Give Alexei an excuse this big and he'll call it off!'

As her mother voiced her daughter's deepest fears Billie shifted uncomfortably in her seat because her conscience was absolutely writhing. It had proved impossible to keep the truth from Lauren once the wedding was being planned and, in some ways, her mother's understanding of Billie's predicament and mood was superior to Hilary's, whose moral compass was less yielding. Lauren totally appreciated that Billie's greatest apprehension was losing the chance to marry the man that she loved. At least if they were married, Billie thought fearfully, she would have the chance to work on the damage she had done to their relationship. Unmarried and living apart, what opportunity would she have to persuade Alexei to calm down and see her viewpoint?

In addition, Lauren saw no reason why her daughter should shoulder all the blame for the fallout caused by Alexei's amnesia. That disastrous accident could not be laid at anyone's door. But Alexei had then swiftly got tangled up with Calisto in what had appeared to be the romance of the century and it was for *his* sake rather than her own that Billie had remained silent. Her mother had deemed that decision 'plain stupidity'.

'Right now, Billie has to keep quiet and save her big announcement about Nicky for when they're married,' Lauren declared in a tone of flat conviction. 'Having carried on the pretence this long, what do another few days matter?'

'What matters is that Billie's relationship with Alexei has changed beyond recognition since he proposed,' Hilary argued vehemently. 'And if she doesn't tell him now, it'll make her look calculating.'

Torn apart by the discussion, Billie went into her bedroom where the beautiful embroidered wedding gown she had purchased in Athens hung in readiness for her wedding day, which was now only forty-eight hours away. She had prayed that Alexei would recall the night they had spent together without her interference. While

she had been in Athens she had even consulted a psy-
chiatrist about Alexei's amnesia. She had received cold
comfort in response. Alexei's memory had only mis-
placed a few hours of the very distressing day when he
had buried his parents. Some day he might recall those
hours or missing fragments of them, but the longer time
went on, the less likely that would be. Furthermore,
filling in that gap in his memory for him was unlikely
to help him to recall events for himself.

In truth, Billie didn't need anyone to tell her what she
ought to do. She knew that with every day that passed
she was sinking deeper into the quagmire of her own deception. She already knew what was right and what was
wrong. She knew the difference. She had no fancy
excuses to hide behind. *Tell him,* a little voice shrieked
in her conscience, but she had seen very little of Alexei
since he had asked her to marry him and what she had
to say could scarcely be passed on during a phone conversation. He was due back at the villa for dinner that
very evening. Once again Billie began mustering her
courage in an effort to bite the bullet and confess all.

Garbed in a dark green knee-length strappy silk
dress, Billie walked into the Drakos villa. Anatalya
greeted her with warmth. While Billie was not quite as
popular as an island girl born and bred on Speros would
have been as Alexei's future bride, she was the nearest
equivalent and, as far as the locals were concerned, in-
finitely preferable to a stranger. Billie glanced at her reflection in a tall mirror. She had done a fair amount of
shopping in Athens, recognising that Alexei expected
her to dress up for her new role in his life. For a young

woman who had once had no particular interest in fashion or her appearance, she had made a big effort. Her hair was trimmed into a more sleek style and her nails were manicured.

Anything to make herself more attractive, anything to please, she ruminated with a frown of growing self-loathing. She had once thought that her appearance didn't matter that much. Now, instead, she thought of Calisto and her well-groomed predecessors and cringed at her naivety. A homespun unadorned woman was unlikely to appeal for very long to a male with Alexei's sophisticated tastes. His standards had to become hers.

That same week she had signed a pre-nuptial contract that ran to fifty pages of small type. She had given up on reading it about halfway through, having only registered that Alexei was promising to give her an enormous allowance every month. Lauren had urged her to consult a lawyer in Athens but Billie preferred to trust the guy she was about to marry and in any case there really wasn't enough time left before the wedding to start negotiating clauses.

As Billie recognised the sound of a helicopter flying in over the bay, she drew in a steadying breath. She was going to do the right thing: she was going to tell him and bear the consequences, whatever they were. She was not a coward. She was not by nature a liar either.

Alexei stared across the big airy salon at his bride-to-be. The green colour of the dress threw her white alabaster skin into prominence and accentuated her jewelled eyes. How had he ever believed she wasn't beau-

tiful? How had he ever considered that vibrant coppery
hair unattractive? Smooth wine-red wings of hair
curving to her cheekbones, eyes bright, mouth a sultry
peachy pink, she looked amazing. He extended a hand
to her in invitation.

'I—I thought I should give you the chance to change
your mind if you want to…about marrying me,' Billie
stammered nervously as she crossed the room to his side.

'I haven't the slightest intention of changing my
mind, *moraki mou*,' Alexei fielded, his wide sensual
mouth flashing an amused smile as he closed a hand
over hers and strode across the hall and down the
bedroom corridor. 'I'm very pleased with the decision
I've made. I also authorised a press release about our engagement today. We'll have a peaceful wedding day.
Unless one of my relatives blabbers, which is of course
possible, the press won't be expecting us to get hitched
so quickly after the announcement.'

Having entered his bedroom, Alexei released her and
jerked loose his tie. 'I need a shower before dinner. Tell
me about your week.'

'There's so much important stuff that we haven't
talked about, Alexei,' Billie said apprehensively, ma-
rooned in the centre of the carpet in the large room.

Shrugging off his jacket and embarking on the
buttons on his shirt, Alexei strolled with predatory grace
towards her. 'We have the rest of our lives to talk. This
marriage is going to last. My aunt, Marina, sends her
best wishes. She approves of you; she said she didn't
know I had so much sense.'

'I'm flattered…'

'Then try to be a little less insecure,' Alexei advised drily. 'I'm not good with needy women.'

In receipt of that criticism, Billie reddened unhappily and stiffened. 'We haven't even discussed… er…having children…'

Alexei quirked a questioning brow, brilliant bronzed eyes pinned to her. 'Some day, but *not* some day soon. I don't want children for a few years yet,' he confided without hesitation.

The opening she had sought had suffered a landslide, cutting her off from that particular route. Right now Alexei didn't want to be a father, which was fair enough because he still thought that he had a choice to exercise on that score. Only he didn't have a choice, which was not a position he was used to occupying. She pictured Nicky, a healthy, livewire baby already learning to grab at objects and roll over while babbling in his own language. She adored her son, believing like all mothers that her baby was the very epitome of cuteness and appeal. It had never occurred to her that Alexei might react to the news that he had a child in a less than positive way and now as that risk did occur to her it glued her tongue to the roof of her mouth. What courage she had built up was steadily draining away.

Alexei's shrewd gaze narrowed. 'I just said the wrong thing, didn't I? Are you really gasping to reproduce?'

'No…er…no. It's not that.' Billie moved restively round the room in no particular direction.

Bare chested, his magnificent torso as well honed by his daily gym workouts as any athlete's, Alexei moved into her path, his hands closing over hers to hold her entrapped and draw her to him. 'Good. Just the two of us appeals the most to me at present. Babies cry and demand a lot of attention,' he pointed out, his breath fanning her cheek before he took her soft lips with ravishing force and urgency.

Her heart went bumpety-bumpety-bump, as if she were running up a steep hill and breathing were a desperate challenge but she didn't want what she was feeling to stop—no, indeed. His hands released hers to search out more sensitive places and she strained eagerly against him as he pushed up the hem of her dress and ran long fingers up the inside of one slender thigh.

A violent trembling seized hold of Billie. Alexei groaned with hungry satisfaction when he reached the stretched taut silk barrier of her knickers and felt the responsive dampness there. He lifted his dark head, his black hair tousled by her clutching fingers, and told her exactly what he wanted to do to her. Her eyes widened in sheer shock at that bold and graphic description.

Engaged in teasing the hot, throbbing sensitivity of the silken flesh between her thighs, Alexei stilled only when he saw her expression. He felt like a firework ready to blaze a trail. She got him hotter and harder than any woman had in a long time and denying himself satisfaction was a challenge until he saw the surprised and self-conscious look on her face. Her lack of experience touched and shamed him. He wanted to give her more than a quick lusty coupling before dinner. Slowly, he withdrew his hand from her seductively responsive flesh and dropped the hem of her dress. He held her close while the after quivers of unsated arousal continued to make her slender frame tremble feverishly against his.

'Alexei…?' she framed, weak-legged with need.

'We have an agreement, *moraki mou*,' he reminded her when she gazed up at him in a daze of confusion. 'We'll wait. It'll be better for you that way…more special.'

Flushed and still shaken when he walked away from her into the bathroom, Billie breathed in deep. She would have lain down on his bed even without an invitation. Her body was a seething mass of pleading nerve-endings, greedily seeking the pleasure that he had given her before. Her face burned with mortification. Even sex, she suddenly appreciated, would now be a risky venture for her. He believed that their wedding night would be 'special'. Did that mean that he was expecting her to be a virgin? It seemed that he did. Would he be able to tell the difference? Was she fated to have to tell the truth to him on their wedding night? *Oh, what a tangled web,* she thought miserably.

Over the meal, served out on the terrace to take advantage of the glorious view of the bay, Alexei asked her a question that startled her. 'One of my relatives asked me who your father was and I realised that I knew nothing on that score.'

Billie tensed. 'Well, you know about as much as I do. Lauren once told me I was the result of a one-night stand with a man she didn't stay in touch with. There's no name on my birth certificate. I'm not sure if Lauren even knew his name,' she admitted in a wry undertone. 'So I didn't push her for any more information.'

Alexei talked business and then, with some amusement, described the calls he had received from curious relations as word of the wedding invitations, made by telephone for discretion, began to spread round the family circle.

'I'm sure that everybody thinks that you could have done much better by marrying a celebrity or an heiress or someone more—'

A fiery glitter in his dark golden eyes, Alexei covered her clenched fingers with his. 'More...*what*? You suit me. How many other women would tolerate me being away for so long without complaint? Ask me intelligent questions about my work and then settle for a quiet dinner at home?'

A deep dark pain pierced her. 'What if I'm not who you think I am, Alexei?' she asked him sickly.

A sinfully magnetic smile slanted his beautifully modelled mouth. 'Then you'll have to work at *being* who I think you are. Stop looking for trouble.'

Billie knew that her wedding day was supposed to be one of the happiest days of her life.

The sky was blue, the sun was shining and the only sound apart from birdsong was the timeless beat of the waves on the white seashore far below. She had her breakfast on the terrace with Nicky in his high chair beside her and marvelled that she could have spent so long building a property that she was only actually going to have lived in for three months. Of course, Hilary planned to stay on and write her book in Billie's house.

'What a gorgeous day!' her aunt carolled, strolling out to join her niece and grand-nephew in the sunshine.

The hours that followed were incredibly busy ones. A beautician and her assistant arrived to do Billie's make-up and her hair, which was to be worn loose the way Alexei said he liked it. Surrendering to their combined attentions, Billie sank into her own little world of thoughts. Speculative articles about her containing few actual facts had already appeared in the world's press and the media had chosen to depict her as a working Cinderella, a little office girl who had miraculously attracted the attention of one of the world's richest and most successful tycoons. Mercifully, none of Lauren's previous lovers had been dug up to tell embarrassing tales and virtually nothing was known about Lauren and Billie's life on the island of Speros. Again, fortunately, the islanders were highly unlikely to sell stories that might embarrass Alexei.

Mid-morning, Billie paused before she donned her sleek simple gown to open the wedding gifts Alexei had sent her. A flat box opened to display a breathtaking diamond pendant and drop earrings. Lauren was ecstatic on her daughter's behalf but Billie felt guiltier than ever. The second box, a good deal bulkier, squirmed as if something inside it were struggling to get out. Eyes wide, Billie lifted the lid and scooped out a little wriggly hairy bundle with four legs and a curling tail and a pair of anxious big brown eyes that could have melted granite. It was a little black Scottish Highland terrier pup.

'What's he doing, giving you a dog?' her mother demanded, unimpressed, indeed checking out the box minutely to ensure it did not contain something more valuable than an animal.

But, of all of them, Billie understood exactly why she was being given a very cute little puppy. It was to satisfy the keen maternal instincts that sixth sense had warned Alexei his bride was concealing. No, he definitely wasn't ready for a baby and he had decided that giving a dog to Billie to dote on as a substitute was a good idea.

'Can you take her with you on your honeymoon?' Hilary asked dubiously.

'I'll call her Skye and I wouldn't dream of leaving her behind.' But a sense of irony swiftly assailed Billie and doused her amusement. Wasn't she about to leave her beloved son behind? That was that, enough was enough, she conceded fiercely. Tonight she would tell Alexei that he was a father. There would be no more pretence, no more excuses, no more put-offs. Whatever happened, she would tell the truth. Her conscience cried that she should never have lied in the first place and she suppressed that voice.

Everything would work out, she told herself urgently. He would come around once he realised he had a son. He would understand why she had remained silent, why she had felt forced to pretend that Nicky was her aunt's child rather than her own, wouldn't he?

So, she wasn't perfect. So, maybe she hadn't done the right thing. So, maybe she had made the wrong choice, had lacked the backbone to go for the tougher option. But she could still remember the tall handsome boy she had first met on the beach all those years earlier when she was being bullied and she reminded herself that Alexei was no innocent when it came to human nature. He would be very surprised by what she had to tell him but she was convinced that he would recognise why she hadn't spoken up sooner.

The wedding ceremony was to take place at the church devoted to *Agios Georgios* down by the harbour in the village. The richly decorated building, built by Alexei's grandfather and packed with guests, was filled with white heavily perfumed flowers and glowing candles that lit the shadows. It was really beautiful and Billie's heart swelled along with the organ music when she saw Alexei waiting at the altar for her. Tall, dark and stunningly handsome with his black-lashed dark golden eyes intent on her, he sent her heart rate rocketing and stole the breath from her lungs.

The religious ceremony was as uplifting for Billie as the wonderful music. She was in love and on a high of positive thoughts. Alexei slid the slender band of gold onto her wedding finger and she rewarded him with a blindingly bright smile. He stared down into her animated happy face and believed that unlike his father he had hit the jackpot the first time around in choosing the right woman to marry. He thought of Calisto's pleading phone call the day before, urging him to change his mind. He had had no time for her interference. No male moved on more quickly from a dead love affair than Alexei.

Billie rested her hand on Alexei's sleeve as they walked back down the aisle. The deed was done: they were married. The man she loved beyond bearing was finally hers to love, her husband. She told herself that it was a day in which to glory in her good fortune and happiness. As he swung her into his arms on the steps to kiss her with breathtaking sensuality and their guests cheered that unashamed display she buried every negative thought and fear and kissed him back with all her heart. He would understand. For her sake and that of their son, he *had* to understand…

HARLEQUIN *Presents*

Coming Next Month

Coming Next Month

LARGER-PRINT BOOKS!

GET 2 FREE LARGER-PRINT
NOVELS PLUS 2 FREE GIFTS!

HARLEQUIN®

A Romance

FOR EVERY MOOD™

Spotlight on

Classic

Quintessential, modern love stories
that are romance at its finest.

See the next page
to enjoy a sneak peek from
the Harlequin® Romance series.

*See below for a sneak peek from our classic
Harlequin® Romance® line.*

Introducing DADDY BY CHRISTMAS by Patricia Thayer.

MIA caught sight of Jarrett when he walked into the open lobby. It was hard not to notice the man. In a charcoal business suit with a crisp white shirt and striped tie covered by a dark trench coat, he looked more Wall Street than small-town Colorado.

Mia couldn't blame him for keeping his distance. He was probably tired of taking care of her.

Besides, why would a man like Jarrett McKane be interested in her? Why would he want to take on a woman expecting a baby? Yet he'd done so many things for her. He'd been there when she'd needed him most. How could she not care about a man like that?

Heart pounding in her ears, she walked up behind him. Jarrett turned to face her. "Did you get enough sleep last night?"

"Yes, thanks to you," she said, wondering if he'd thought about their kiss. Her gaze went to his mouth, then she quickly glanced away. "And thank you for not bringing up my meltdown."

Jarrett couldn't stop looking at Mia. Blue was definitely her color, bringing out the richness of her eyes.

"What meltdown?" he said, trying hard to focus on what she was saying. "You were just exhausted from lack of sleep and worried about your baby."

He couldn't help remembering how, during the night, he'd kept going in to watch her sleep. How strange was that? "I hope you got enough rest."

She nodded. "Plenty. And you're a good neighbor for

coming to my rescue."

He tensed. Neighbor? *What neighbor kisses you like I did?* "That's me, just the full-service landlord," he said, trying to keep the sarcasm out of his voice. He started to leave, but she put her hand on his arm.

"Jarrett, what I meant was you went beyond helping me." Her eyes searched his face. "I've asked far too much of you."

"Did you hear me complain?"

She shook her head. "You should. I feel like I've taken advantage."

"Like I said, I haven't minded."

"And I'm grateful for everything…"

Grasping her hand on his arm, Jarrett leaned forward. The memory of last night's kiss had him aching for another. "I didn't do it for your gratitude, Mia."

Gorgeous tycoon Jarrett McKane has never believed in Christmas—but he can't help being drawn to soon-to-be-mom Mia Saunders! Christmases past were spent alone…and now Jarrett may just have a fairy-tale ending for all his Christmases future!

Available December 2010, only from Harlequin® Romance®.

SILHOUETTE
SPECIAL EDITION

USA TODAY BESTSELLING AUTHOR

MARIE FERRARELLA

BRINGS YOU ANOTHER
HEARTWARMING STORY FROM

❦MATCHMAKING
Mamas

When Lilli McCall disappeared on him
after he proposed, Kullen Manetti swore
never to fall in love again. Eight years later
Lilli is back in his life, threatening to break
down all the walls he's put up to
safeguard his heart.

UNWRAPPING
THE PLAYBOY

*Available December
wherever books are sold.*

HARLEQUIN *Presents*

Bestselling Harlequin Presents® author

Julia James

brings you her most powerful book yet...

FORBIDDEN OR
FOR BEDDING?

The shamed mistress...

Guy de Rochemont's name is a byword for wealth
and power—and now his duty is to wed.

Alexa Harcourt knows she can never be anything
more than *The de Rochemont Mistress*.

But Alexa—the one woman Guy wants—is also
the one woman whose reputation
forbids him to take her as his wife....

**Available from Harlequin Presents
December 2010**